HELLION'S JOURNEY
A HELLION HOUSE NOVELLA

EMMA JANE HOLLOWAY

HELLION'S JOURNEY

When home is anything but a haven ...

Detective Inspector Palmer yearns for a caseload of ordinary crimes—no monsters, no mages, and definitely no magic. Dark sorcery has left his city in bloody chaos, and Palmer is exhausted. But then Layla, one of the beauties from the notorious Hellion House, darkens his interrogation room door.

Lovely Layla is more welcome in Palmer's daydreams, where her obsession for silver bullets and sharp knives can be safely ignored. But now she brings news about his most-wanted villain —the mechanic responsible for sabotaging the *Leopard* and sending most of the airship's crew to a fiery death.

The evidence points to Palmer's home town—a rough-and-ready hellhole he'd gratefully left behind. Now, with Layla at his side, he returns to his birthplace, and to the scene of a half-forgotten murder. All at once, his freedom, his mission, and Layla's safety depend on solving the cold case. That's no mean feat in a town full of crooks, drifters, and broken-down magicians, but DI Palmer always catches his culprit.

Until now. Uncovering one deadly secret is sure to reveal others—including his own.

CHAPTER 1

*D*etective Inspector Palmer was momentarily content. It was a sunny afternoon, warmer than it should have been for March, and for the first time in months, Londria's criminals had run short on imagination. There were no buildings melting to puddles of slag and magefire, no exploding airships, and no armies of flesh-eating Unseen cavorting in the streets. After months of unrest, the city had settled into a new rhythm. Peace would not last, but he'd enjoy it while he could.

The promise of spring had brought out the crowds. Even Palmer had seized the opportunity to get out from behind his desk. There were plenty of half-forgotten cases needing some legwork, and the sunshine beckoned. With luck, he might be able to end his day with a quiet drink at the Mercury Café.

But Palmer was not a lucky man. Just then, he spotted the young woman walking a dozen yards ahead of him. The milling crowd almost hid her slim back and the feathered hat perched atop her upswept strawberry-blond curls. He blinked, hoping he had seen a mirage, but alas. There was no mistaking the sway of her bustle and the flash of red leather boot heels beneath her black-and-white striped skirts.

Layla McHugh was a problem the way a craving for strong whisky was a problem—unhelpful, best avoided, and only reluctantly discussed. But she was intoxicating, even from a carefully maintained distance.

Palmer slowed his steps, his stomach tight with anxiety. Where was she bound and why? Layla was widely acknowledged as the reigning beauty of Hellion House, one of Londria's more exclusive brothels. Both she and her employer, the infamous Mrs. Randall, were up to their beribboned garters in the city's social and political intrigues. Complicated trouble followed Layla like the scent of her lemony perfume. She'd even got herself mixed up with the Anathema Club, a mob of vigilante monster-slayers, although he couldn't quite picture her with a bloody sword in one hand.

He stopped to study the wares in the tobacconist's shop window, letting the woman get ahead. Perhaps she'd go about her business and vanish out of his, taking her cloud of chaos with her. But then she took a right turn into the Wordsworth Jewelry and Fine Silver Emporium. Knowing Layla's love of shiny, thievable trinkets, one might as well open the fishmonger's door to an enterprising cat. Palmer followed, the afternoon warmth no longer a balm to his mood.

By the time he reached the jeweler's door, Layla stood at the glass-topped counter inside, pointing to a necklace with one white-gloved finger. From the proprietor's harried expression, this wasn't her first request to inspect some bauble up close. She gave a guilty start when she saw Palmer's reflection in the glass, then offered a disarming smile.

"Detective Inspector," she said in a voice like warm honey. She had a way of gazing up at a man that made Palmer's sober-hued waistcoat feel too tight.

"Miss McHugh," Palmer said as he came to a stop at her side. "And Mr. Wordsworth, a pleasure as always."

"Good day, Mr. Palmer," replied Wordsworth, who watched

Layla with pink-cheeked fascination. Whether his interest was down to a pretty face or the prospect of a sale, Palmer couldn't tell. With Layla, either one was a bad bet.

A tray of rings already sat on the counter. With the tip of her tongue caught between her teeth, Layla reached for the top row of sparklies. Gently but firmly, Palmer caught her hand. For a tortured instant, she studied him from beneath her lashes, her gaze a well of chaos that threatened to drag him under. He released her fingers and stepped back.

"I apologize for interrupting your visit, Miss McHugh," he said with studied politeness. "However, I have a question that requires an immediate response. Perhaps you could join me outside?"

"Of course." A frown of confusion puckered her brow, convincing enough that he almost believed her innocence.

"Will that be everything for today, then, miss?" Wordsworth asked.

"Yes, thank you." Layla picked up her drawstring silk handbag from where she'd set it on the counter and, with a last look around the store, made her exit. With an air of disappointment, Wordsworth returned the tray of rings to its secure spot under glass. Palmer hurried to catch up to Layla and hold the door so she could pass.

"Whatever is the matter, Detective?" she asked, her tone lightly teasing. Outside, the sun turned wisps of her hair to a fiery red. Her gloved fingers rested lightly on his sleeve. "Is this a social encounter, or am I the suspect in a crime?"

Palmer's arm grew warm at her touch—his imagination, no doubt. "You have something I require."

"What might that be?" Her smile promised everything and nothing.

"Come with me." Palmer steered her down the street, out of sight of the jewelers and the flower shop next door.

Layla made no protest, following him as if they were out for an afternoon stroll. Inwardly, Palmer cursed. He had one of the loveliest women in Londria on his arm, one possessed of beauty, wit, and considerable intelligence—and he was in no position to enjoy the moment.

"I suppose you don't get many afternoons to yourself," she said a moment later, tilting her head to give him the whole of her attention.

"Is that what this is?"

She laughed. "We are two grown adults enjoying the fresh air. What would you like this to be?"

Palmer didn't reply. They turned right at the next corner and crossed the busy thoroughfare. From there, he could see the police station at the end of the street. A statue of Athena stood to one side of the double doors, Hercules to the other. Wisdom and strength. Those were virtues Palmer strove for every minute of his working life, and he'd need a double helping with Layla in tow.

At the sight of the station, her steps flagged.

"Wait just one minute." She cast him a sharp look. "You said you required something from me. You didn't say anything about police business."

"No, I didn't."

"I thought—"

It was his turn to smile. "You thought I was off duty and ready for an afternoon of your professional attention."

Her lips drew back, as if she were about to snarl. "As if I would—"

Palmer didn't want to hear the end of that sentence. "It would be to your advantage to come quietly."

Layla's hand slipped from his arm as caution filled her sea-blue eyes. "And if I don't?"

He caught her arm above the elbow, holding her just firmly enough that she couldn't pull away. "It's my understanding that

Mrs. Randall has rules about her ladies engaging in petty thievery. It lowers the tone of her fine establishment."

Layla's mouth dropped open. "What do you—?"

Palmer marched her forward fast enough that she almost tripped. "I ask the questions."

She glared daggers his way. "You've no cause to suspect me. I've never been convicted of anything, much less stealing."

"But you have an impressive file. We might never have locked you up, but we've had plenty of reasons to arrest you."

"All that means is you're bad at your job."

"I will endeavor to do better."

He nodded to two junior detectives loitering by the station's front counter and took Layla directly to a room at the back of the building. It was small and poorly lit, with only a scarred table and two chairs. Most would pick a larger space for an interview, but Palmer found a use for the confined atmosphere. It was a silent reminder of what awaited uncooperative guests.

Palmer ushered Layla to the chair facing the door. She sat, her purse resting in her lap. She seemed to shrink in on herself, as if trying to make as little contact with her surroundings as possible. He pretended not to notice, slowly taking the chair closest to the door. She watched him with a mulish expression, but didn't bother to protest her innocence again. Clearly, she'd been down this road often enough to know better.

He fixed her with a stern glare. "Show me what's in your bag."

Her lips thinned. "What's in a lady's reticule is her own business."

"I doubt there's anything there that will surprise me."

Which was the problem. Women like Layla—often working in pairs—bamboozled shopkeepers out of costly goods every day. He'd seen all their tricks before—the chatter, the smiles, asking to see this and that and, oh, what was the pretty thing on the shelf? What had she taken from Wordsworth during the time he had one tray on the counter and she was pointing to something else under the glass? All the poor fool had to do was glance away for a second and she'd have swept some bauble into that drawstring bag she had sitting on the counter.

Glumly, she set her purse on the counter. It was black silk dotted with white tassels. Palmer pulled open the mouth of the bag and dumped the contents onto the table. Coins, hairpins, a tin of pastilles, a comb, a handkerchief, and a few folded banknotes fell out. So did a wicked looking folding knife with a pearl handle, two discreetly wrapped rubber condoms, and a vial of smelling salts. When he pushed the embroidered handkerchief aside, he found what he was looking for. A ring rolled out of the folds of cloth, light flashing from a small but well-cut emerald.

Palmer picked it up, examining the stone's clarity. Layla's eyebrow twitched, but she remained silent. Palmer set it aside and looked at what else the handkerchief had hidden beneath it.

A silver case no bigger than a calling card lay among the scattered items. The case was heavily engraved with a pattern of vines and flowers. He pressed the catch, and the front sprang open to display a pair of photographs—an older couple in formal clothes. No one he recognized. He pressed the catch again, and a hidden mechanism gave a quiet *whirr-click* and replaced those pictures with new ones—this time a younger couple who might have been newlyweds. Another click, and two more faces. And two more after that before it cycled back to the originals. The gallery case was a clever piece of work, for the entire device was no more than a quarter of an inch thick. Palmer snapped it shut and studied the maker's mark stamped on the back.

It was shaped like a pair of shears—the type used for fleecing sheep. The design was familiar, down to the hexagon surrounding the shears. Memories flooded Palmer, making his limbs go cold. He set the case on the table with a soft clunk.

"You look like you've seen a ghost," Layla said, sounding almost concerned.

"Why this device?" Palmer asked, ignoring the remark. "It is a fascinating toy, but there were far more valuable items on display."

She shrugged one shoulder. "I paid for that, right and proper. You can ask Mr. Wordsworth."

"I will," he replied, though he believed her on this point. "And I will ask him about the ring as well."

A flood of pink suffused Layla's cheeks, confirming his suspicion that the ring had come from the tray on Wordsworth's counter. She'd probably swept it up at the same time as the legitimate purchase and deposited both into her bag at once. One flutter of her eyelashes, and the jeweler would have been fixated on her face, not her hands.

Chaos. The woman was chaos.

Palmer turned back to the gallery case. "Why does your mistress want this particular item?"

Layla stiffened. "I never said anything about Mrs. R."

"Tell me the truth, or I'll tell her what else you took from that shop. She doesn't allow her girls to steal and, from what I can tell, she doesn't take disobedience well. You'll be working on street corners instead of the fine chambers of Hellion House."

That might have been an overstatement, or not. Either way, the color left Layla's cheeks. She leaned across the table. "Listen. She had her reasons for wanting the case. You know she has her ways for finding things out. Always for a good reason, of course."

"Of course." Somehow, Palmer kept a straight face. Hellion House entertained the politicians, aristocrats, and industrial barons in Londria. Mrs. Randall had a literal finger—or another intimate body part—on every important pulse in town. "Go on."

"You remember when the *Leopard* blew up?"

"A large airship exploding over the city was somewhat hard to miss."

Layla's eyes narrowed at his jibe. "Well, she thinks that case belonged to the man who sabotaged the ship."

Palmer froze. If she was right, this was fresh evidence on a high-profile unsolved case. Outside of a few survivor accounts—a handful of aeronauts had survived the catastrophe—there had been little to investigate. There were reports of tampering, stolen plans, and a delivery that might have been made by the saboteur. None had given him a name or a description, and he salivated for the taste of a real clue.

It was more than just another crime. His friend, Gideon Fletcher, belonged to the family who'd built the ship. Gideon's sister, Miranda, had barely escaped the incident with her life. Palmer's inability to close the case felt like a personal failing.

And here was Layla, dangling information like the temptress she was. He could have asked why Mrs. Randall was meddling in the case, but didn't bother. She traded in secrets as much as pleasure, and could have had several motivations. He moved on to a better question, scrubbing any excitement from his voice.

"What makes Mrs. Randall believe this belonged to the suspect? Countless leads turned out to be smoke in the wind."

Layla flicked the gallery case with her finger, making it spin in a lazy circle. "One of her gentleman visitors won it in a card game and then sold it a few days later."

Palmer put a hand over the case, stopping the spin. "Can this gentleman visitor's information be trusted?"

Layla gave a low laugh. "The man who won this pretty toy swims at the shallow end of the political pool. He is an observer of the game without ever touching the pieces. However, I don't doubt his ability to gather gossip. He knows everything said or done in Londria's drawing rooms."

"That doesn't answer my question."

"What are you going to do about the ring?"

"Answer my questions and I will consider alternatives."

She made a face. "That line wouldn't work for anyone but you, Palmer."

"Why me?"

"You never set a foot wrong, even to lie to a whore."

Palmer let the jibe slide past. Enough that she'd take the bargain of leniency in trade for a lead. "Talk."

"I'm not a dog."

"You are suspected of thievery until I say otherwise."

Layla lifted her chin, mouth stubborn.

Palmer cleared his throat, imagining that look combined with fine sheets and candlelight. Desperately, he wrenched his mind back to the straight and narrow. If he lost his footing as a man of law and order, he lost everything he was. "Please continue."

"Fine." She somehow managed to flounce, even when seated. "Our gentleman said the owner of this case was introduced to him as Mr. Polliver. That may or may not be his real name."

"Understood."

She nodded toward the silver object. "Those are your mystery man Polliver's family pictures. One might even be him."

"How do you know that?" A prickle of anticipation ran down the back of his neck. He had a name. Maybe a face. Or maybe nothing.

"Our gentleman sold the case before he changed the images."

"He needed the money." Palmer made it a statement.

Layla shrugged. "He's a dandy. All those club memberships and card games don't come cheaply."

Palmer picked up the case, letting the light from the single window play on its silver surface. For an instant, it reminded him of his younger brother. Kieran would have admired the workmanship. Probably would have tried to replicate it.

Palmer pushed the memory aside. That was a deep, dark rabbit hole he couldn't afford to go down—not now, when he had a job to do. "How does Polliver link to the *Leopard*? What else did your man say?"

"Nothing we didn't already suspect. Polliver was a hireling from somewhere outside Londria—a stranger no one would recognize. He apparently had the skills they needed—explosives, mechanics, experience with magic-enhanced tools for getting the job done fast. Those that paid him didn't like what Fletcher Industries was doing."

The *Leopard* had carried a weapon that kept the Unseen from threatening the city walls. Up until that moment, the mages of the Conclave had been the only defense against the flesh-eating horrors—and had profited greatly from Londria's gratitude. They hadn't appreciated competition from the airship or its maker.

Neither had those who had thrived under the mages' rule. Even now, after the Conclave had been overthrown, there were those who wished the robed bastards would return. Palmer didn't. He knew all about the dungeon in the old Citadel and what the Conclave had done to their prisoners.

He shook off the memory, forcing himself back to the present. "Did your man name the individuals who hired Polliver?"

"No."

"Do you think your informant could find Polliver?"

"No."

"Why not?" Palmer had to find out who had paid the man. The need ached like a dagger through his gut.

She frowned. "Our informant, as you call him, is nowhere to be found. I don't know if that is connected to our inquiry, or not."

Palmer swore. "Then how do I find him?"

Layla sat back in her chair, her earlier unease forgotten. "Word has it he left Londria the morning after the card game. Went back to wherever he came from. No one knows the name of the place."

Palmer turned the case over to stare at the maker's mark. "I do."

"What?" she asked in surprise. "Where?"

"Wilcolme Haven," Palmer replied, his voice flat with emotions he refused to name. No wonder the case had reminded him of the past. *The killer came from my godforsaken home town.*

CHAPTER 2

Palmer escorted Layla to the exit of the police station. It went against the grain to let her go, but he'd made a bargain and word would spread if he broke it. A detective was only as good as his informants. So, as she'd said, he'd keep his end of their deal. Even with her.

A part of him said, *especially with her*. A different, smarter piece of his soul said he'd wished he'd never met the woman. He could resist a pretty face, but there was something in Layla McHugh that undermined his carefully constructed sense of order. She was unruly, almost rudely alive. If he let her, she'd take him apart like a child's puzzle toy and leave the pieces scattered in her wake.

"Behave yourself," he said as he held open the station door. It was a ridiculous thing to say. Of course, she wouldn't. "Remember, I know where to find you. Give Mrs. Randall my compliments."

With a flash of her blue eyes, she bobbed an ironic curtsey. "Good day, Detective Inspector." She swept down the street without a backward glance.

Palmer watched her go with annoyance. He'd given her more

grace than she deserved. Not that she'd ever thank him for it. He thrust his hands in his pockets, fingering the ring and the silver case. If he was honest with himself, he could have locked her up in some dark, secret corner of the cells and sweated the information out of her. But brutality cut both ways—he'd learned that young. He wasn't afraid to use it, but it was the very last tool he'd choose.

He turned his steps toward the administration desk, where he'd put the valuables under lock and key until he could meet with his captain. He had half a mind to visit Wordsworth straight away to confirm that the gallery case was a legitimate purchase, and the ring was not. If he never logged the items into evidence, he could save himself the paperwork—but thought better of it. As his da used to say, once a corner was cut, it was a devil to put back in place.

The memory of his father sent a prickle down his spine. Childhood memories were supposed to be cozy and comforting, but Wilcolme Haven—the forsaken hellhole—had been anything but safe.

Palmer crossed the worn tile floor of the station's entrance. A high wooden counter, where a pair of constables and a desk sergeant dealt with the public, stood to the left. As usual, a dozen members of the public were there demanding attention. The din echoed around the vaulted ceiling, drowning out the noise from the street.

He didn't hear Detective Martindale until the younger officer was standing in his path. "The chief needs you, sir. You've dealt with this sort of thing before."

Palmer stopped short. "Dealt with what?"

Martindale's eyes were glassy with shock. The young officer shook his head, a flicker of panic crossing his face. Palmer put a hand on his shoulder, offering silent support. He'd had a hand in training Martindale, and the lad was solid. Whatever had rattled him had to be bad.

Martindale sucked in a breath, but before he could continue, Captain Sturgess descended the stairs at a run. "Palmer. Whitley. Martindale. Go with DI Murray."

Palmer turned to see Murray standing at the entrance, a rifle held loosely at his side. The man raised the weapon with a grimace. "Arm up. There's some excitement at the Riverside Bazaar."

As he spoke, a large black police wagon drew up outside, pulled by four horses with heavy, feathered feet. Murray meant business. Palmer didn't pause for discussion, but accepted the rifle Whitley handed him and sprinted for the vehicle. It was made for hauling prisoners, with caged windows and two benches facing one another in the back—but it could carry a strike squad equally well. He grabbed the vertical bars on either side of the open back door and sprang inside, the others on his heels. Whitley slammed the door closed, and the wagon lurched forward with a jolt. Murray and Palmer sat on one bench, Whitley and Martindale on the other. Something inside the rig smelled like stale vomit.

"What details do we have? What are we walking into?" Palmer asked.

"Unseen," Murray replied, as if the single word required no further explanation.

In some ways, it didn't. The Unseen were monsters from the forested Outlands beyond Londria's protective walls. Some Unseen were mere shuffling goblins, others of nearly human intelligence. He had it on good authority that some had started out as humans and fallen afoul of the mages. If that was true, the monsters absolutely had their vengeance during the sack of the Citadel. Very few mages had survived.

But Palmer didn't care about the Unseen's origins—not at times like this. What mattered far more was that the thrice-damned horrors ate human flesh and had found a way into the city.

Whitley visibly flinched at the news. "How many this time?"

Martindale answered, his voice thin with strain. "Two. Maybe three. They were holed up in a grocer's stockroom. The shop boy surprised them and they ran."

As a rule, Unseen shunned the sunlight unless there was a chance of an easy kill. Alleys, sheds, and sewers were best avoided, especially in the outskirts of town.

"Is the boy still alive?" Palmer asked.

Martindale gave a quick shake of his head. "Three of the other shopkeepers had firearms. One had a blunderbuss. They were keeping the gnashers pinned down when I went for reinforcements."

Gnashers. It was the latest name for the Unseen. As if a bit of slang could make them less deadly.

Palmer pulled out his watch. "When did you leave the scene?"

"Quarter past two o'clock."

"Seventeen minutes ago."

No one spoke. Martindale had acted with remarkable speed, but a fast response was everything. So was experience. There was a reason Sturgess had sent four of his top men instead of an army who'd never faced the beasts before.

The vehicle jerked to a halt, and in moments they were on the street in front of the Riverside Bazaar. It was located in a small but fashionable shopping district—not as well-to-do as the area around Wordsworth's jewelry store, but nice enough to attract a good clientele. The bazaar was housed inside a long brick building with an arched, iron-framed glass roof. The shops themselves were booths on the ground floor and on a mezzanine level. Palmer had been inside exactly twice, which was enough to remind him how little he liked crowds.

Only now his job was to keep them safe. Whitley and Martindale peeled away, running toward the east end of the building. Murray and Palmer took the doors to the west. They approached slowly, Palmer in the lead and hugging the side of the building.

He ducked beneath the windows as he passed them, careful to stay out of sight.

The entrance was framed in polished oak with etched glass panels and brass hardware—an expensive look that, in Palmer's experience, matched the prices inside. Palmer slowed as he approached, noting that the doors were ajar, propped open by something on the ground. He held up a hand, signaling Murray to halt. Inching closer, he saw what looked like a bundle of fabric caught between the doors. Cautiously, he pulled the closest door open, rifle at the ready. The bundle shifted, flopping against the stone tiles of the entryway.

It was a leg, still in its gray flannel trousers. Palmer edged around the door to discover the rest—or three-quarters of the rest—of a man. Probably a patron, based on the quality of the clothes. Heart pounding, Palmer circled the body, not bothering to check for signs of life. The head and one arm were missing.

Murray joined Palmer, silently surveying the scene. At first glance, the building and its shops seemed deserted. The wide central aisle was empty except for the huge potted plants that thrived beneath the glass roof. Most of the patrons would have fled, but he was willing to bet a few were hiding beneath shop tables and behind the velvet curtains that separated one stall from the next. He could feel their terror like cold fingers against his skin.

"Where to first?" Palmer asked, the words barely above a whisper.

"Main floor, then up, quick and quiet."

They began moving at a fast walk, Palmer angling his rifle to the left, Murray covering the right. They'd both performed this maneuver countless times over the last months. Ever since the Conclave fell, no mages reinforced the city walls with the magic that kept the Unseen at bay. The monsters made regular forays into Londria to hunt, though rarely this far into the city's core. They were getting bolder.

Sweat trickled between Palmer's shoulder blades. Danger sharpened every sensation, from the smooth weight of the rifle against his shoulder to the crunch of grit against the polished floor. This was the kind of cluttered environment he hated, with too many places for the enemy to hide. His gaze flicked from the market stalls to his left, to the mezzanine above, to the ceiling, to the sweep of the staircase that connected the two levels. He flinched as an air current stirred the leaves of a potted palm.

A face suddenly appeared, peering from beneath a table loaded with perfumes. Palmer swung the rifle. The figure recoiled, like a mouse vanishing into its hole. A moment later, the young female slowly reappeared, mouth flattened into a grim line. A shop girl—very human—and pale with fear. Palmer shook his head, willing her to vanish again. Instead, she pointed toward the stairs that led up to the mezzanine and silently mouthed, *That way.*

Palmer signaled to Murray, and they angled toward the stairs. He could hear movement ahead. Whitley and Martindale? He managed to keep hoping until they came around the graceful arc of the marble staircase and saw what lay on the other side.

A foul-smelling mass of entrails, hair, and what might have been a shopkeeper's smock blocked the foot of the steps. It was impossible to tell anything more about the figure, other than it had worn the kind of half-boots fashionable with young girls. A glistening red trail smeared the stairway, splatters of crimson catching the light from the mezzanine windows.

"What do you make of that?" Murray asked softly, his steel-gray eyes fixed on the gore.

"Someone got hungry."

Murray blanched another degree. "Gods help us."

"The gods have turned their backs," Palmer muttered. "That's why they called us."

Nausea—and a good deal of fear—eddied in Palmer's gut as he crept up the stairs, rifle at the ready. The mezzanine was a wide balcony wrapped around the central atrium of the building, allowing enough space for a second floor of booths. An ornate iron railing kept shoppers safe from a steep fall to the marble floor below. He tried to gather more details, but the stink of the corpse's discarded guts clogged the back of his throat. He swallowed hard, but the urge to retch hovered. He had to push it aside, concentrate harder. His life—his team's life—depended on every member staying sharp.

Murray followed a step behind, moving backward to cover their rear. He fell in beside Palmer when they reached the top. Immediately ahead were three men. The two with rifles wore the uniform of hired security guards. The third was a heavy-set shopkeeper with a blunderbuss. It was a strange weapon—barely two feet long, with a wide muzzle that sprayed shot with a mere nod to accuracy. Probably a family heirloom, kept in the shop for show until today.

All three men were aiming at something in the nearest stall. Palmer and Murray edged forward, their own weapons raised. A display table had tipped over, scattering bottles and bundles of herbs. The booth's curtains, garlanded with silver paper moons and stars, were drawn tight.

"We're from Gryphon Avenue," Palmer announced to the gunmen. The street name was synonymous with the police headquarters.

The man with the blunderbuss cast them a sideways look, jowls trembling. "About time. The gnashers are in there."

"How many?"

"Three." The man blinked rapidly. "Plus my shop boy."

"You're the grocer?" Murray asked.

"Fenniwell."

Of course. Fenniwell's Fine Emporium. The kind of place that sold spices Palmer hadn't heard of and could never afford. "Anyone else? Whose shop is this?"

"Over there." The grocer nodded toward the rail that circled the mezzanine.

A black-haired woman in a gauzy dress slumped against the balcony rail, her face slack with shock. One of the potion bottles from the booth dangled from her lace-gloved hand. She stood so still, he hadn't noticed her until now. "Madam, please leave the area at once. It's not safe."

A noise—something between a grunt and a snarl—emerged from the booth. Palmer drew level with the grocer, aiming at the velvet curtains. They swayed slightly, showing someone—or thing—was moving inside. The grocer was starting to shake, his finger unsteady on the trigger of his antique weapon.

"How did this start?" Palmer asked Fenniwell, hoping the question would quiet the man's nerves—and maybe his own. He felt sweat trickle down his back even though his limbs felt bloodless.

Murray came up on Palmer's left, his own face shiny with perspiration.

"They were in the back room," Fenniwell said in a strangled voice. "I sent Lewis for a jar of pickled mushrooms. They shot out of the dark like demons from Hell."

"And Lewis?"

"Didn't make a sound. They just took him."

And now the Unseen were cornered. Unusual for such cunning creatures. These specimens were either overconfident or inexperienced, but without the magic of the Conclave, anything could get inside the city. A sudden vision of Layla McHugh walking alone through the streets made his fear run to thick, hot anger.

Feet pounded up the stairs, distracting him. It was Martindale, with a gray-faced Whitley two steps behind. The lad looked like he was about to faint.

"Palmer?" Martindale called. "Murray?"

"Over here," Palmer called back. He sucked in a breath. With two more guns, they stood a chance. He turned to Fenniwell. "There's only one way this ends. Coordinated fire."

"We can't," Fennel said quickly, a quaver in his voice. "The boy's in there."

For a fleeting moment, Palmer wondered who Lewis was to this man. Maybe not a son, but the lad was clearly like a son. Then the sound of rending flesh came from behind the curtain.

"He's not coming back."

Something snapped behind Fenniwell's eyes. A ruddy flush swept up his cheeks. Without warning, he charged forward. Palmer grabbed for the man, but Fenniwell's sleeve slipped through his grasp. The grocer thrust the muzzle of the blunderbuss through the curtains and fired with an earsplitting *blam*.

Smoke billowed, followed by an inhuman shriek of rage. Murray screamed an ear-splitting curse as all three unseen shot from behind the curtain, fangs bared. Rifles thundered, the noise echoing around the high ceiling. One bullet hit the rod holding the velvet curtain, sending a flare of sparks and metal shards into the air.

A weight hit Palmer in the chest. He fell backward, hitting the marble floor hard. Pain shot down his spine, and the rifle slipped from his grasp. Clawed hands wrapped around his throat as he struggled to clear his vision. An Unseen straddled his chest, crushing the air from his body. This was one of the ugly ones, shriveled, pale, and hairless like something found in a bottomless cave. Palmer gagged as folds of its tattered shirt dragged across his face, leaving a trail of gritty filth in its wake. It stank of rotten meat.

He bucked, desperate for air. The thing hissed, lips drawing back from a mouth smeared with red and crammed with too many needle-sharp fangs. Breath and spittle splattered his face as the thing bent to look Palmer in the eye. Blood trickled down the side of its head where a rifle bullet had creased its scalp.

The creature caught his gaze, and the snarl turned into a snaggletoothed grin. "M-m-missssed."

Blackness edged Palmer's vision as the Unseen tightened its grip. His hand shot to the side, groping for his rifle. Closed around something else. Breathed in a huge gulp of air as the creature let go and pinned his shoulders instead. Saliva glistened on its chin as its fangs gaped wide.

Palmer struck, stabbing whatever he'd grabbed into the side of the creature's neck. The Unseen made a gargling squawk, its colorless eyes going wide with surprise. Then warm liquid gloved Palmer's hand. The thing shuddered, then flopped limply across Palmer's body, neck still gushing a dark crimson stream.

Palmer shoved the body roughly aside, revulsion taking over. He sprang to his feet, uncurling his fingers to find he'd grabbed a piece of the shattered curtain rod. The ragged end had sliced through an artery. He flung the shard away, scattering a shower of Unseen blood. His gorge rose, but a movement behind him made him spin, automatically snatching up his lost rifle from the marble tile.

One of the security guards was on his knees, an Unseen female in the act of ripping away his firearm. She looked almost human, her long white hair floating around an oval face. Pretty, except for the fangs. She raised the rifle, about to club the guard. Palmer shot her through the skull. Two down.

Martindale grappled with the third—another of the hunched, hairless ones—and was losing badly. One of the detective's arms hung loose, probably broken. Palmer couldn't get a clean shot. He stepped to the left, trying to get a better position when something flew past his ear, gleaming like a rogue star. It smashed against the balcony rail, sending up a fountain of glass and clear liquid.

Martindale twisted away, agile as an eel, but the Unseen was coated by the spray. It reeled, arms wide and claws extended, as if groping blindly for its prey. It fell hard against the balcony rail, feet leaving the ground, and burst into flames. The creature teetered for a moment, the blue-white flame roaring like sails in the wind, before it toppled and fell to the floor below. Someone on the ground floor screamed.

Palmer sprang to the rail and looked over. The flames were orange now, sputtering from a pile of charred bones. The creature had fallen onto a blank stretch of the marble floor. The fire wouldn't spread. He exhaled, feeling suddenly weak.

A flutter of gauzy fabric made him look up. It was the fortune teller. Up close, he could see the delicate facial tattoos that marked her as one of the River Rats—nomads who sailed the waters beyond the city's walls.

She flicked her dark gaze his way, then pointed to the floor below. "The hunters are gone and the birds return." Her voice was low, tinged by her people's distinctive accent.

He followed her gesture and saw Londrians—merchants, customers, and a few of the scruffy children who were everywhere on the streets—crawling out from under tables and behind screens. A low murmur of voices began to gather strength.

"You threw that bottle," he said.

"Of course," she said. "Like you, I will play my part in any fight."

It was an odd statement, as if they were old acquaintances. He let it pass. "What was in the bottle?"

She brushed her hair from her face, fingers shaking. "I'm not sure. I picked up the first one I could find and told it to do its duty."

Palmer opened his mouth to ask more questions, but she turned away. A moment later, she was bending over Martindale, who had sunk to the floor. After a few words, she began examining his arm.

Palmer shook himself. He had victims to attend to—or thought he did, until he began looking around. Whitley was nowhere in sight, which was worrying. Murray was giving orders to the growing crowd to keep away from the scene. He had a bloody cut over one eye, and his arm was swathed in makeshift bandages that looked suspiciously like tablecloths from the displays. One of the security men was also mobile, but the other was dead. Most of Fenniwell's chest was missing. A glance inside the velvet booth with its silver stars revealed what was left of Lewis. With a flinch, Palmer backed away.

It was always this way with the monsters. His team—the humans—had been too late, too sure of themselves, and far too few. They'd failed—or he had. If he'd been faster, a better shot, more would have survived. Martindale would not be white-faced and sweating as the fortune-teller bound up his arm.

Palmer knelt beside him. "You did well."

The young man's eyes were wide with pain. "I nearly ran."

The fortune teller made a calming noise, casting Palmer a dark look for upsetting her patient.

"Is that what happened to Whitley?" Palmer asked, ignoring the woman.

Martindale closed his eyes and gave an almost imperceptible nod.

"It happens," Palmer said easily. "Reasonable men do their best to stay alive."

"Not like us." The lad sounded bitter.

"Exactly." Palmer rose. "Rest there."

He walked away, head full of what he had to do next. Find a surgeon. Take statements. Move the bodies. Notify kin. He'd be up all night. A throbbing ache was taking over his body one muscle at a time, reminding him he'd been in a brutal fight. When he reached the top of the stairs, the fortune teller caught up to him.

"Were you bitten?" she asked, eying his blood-soaked clothes.

He shook his head, wishing he could tear off the stinking garments. They were starting to go stiff as the blood dried.

"Good. Their bite poisons the blood." Without asking permission, she took his left arm and peeled back the blood-soaked sleeve. The creature's claws had scored the flesh deeply enough that the woman caught her breath. "You did not come away whole."

Palmer turned away, not wanting to look. "I'll have a surgeon stitch that up."

"Do what you feel you must," she replied, pressing a cloth to the wound.

It was soaked with something that stung like the devil. Palmer hissed in pain, but didn't try to pull away. The River Rats had survived in the Outlands for centuries. He trusted their medicine. "Is it bad?"

"Better than most here."

Something sharp pressed into his skin, but when he looked, it was not a needle. It looked more like a stylus, and as she moved the implement around the wound, it left a pattern of inky marks.

"What is that?" he asked.

"This will close the wound and keep it clean."

He wanted to ask how—the marks looked like a swirling script, not evidence of a medical procedure.

"You will recover quickly, which will be necessary." She said it as if his continued health were a matter of her own convenience. "You have unfinished business. A journey to make."

"I do?" A wave of fatigue battled his curiosity and won—almost.

"You came when I needed you," she said. "Reading your future was the least I could do."

He made a noise that might have been a laugh. "And that's all you saw?"

She gave him another sideways glance. "Beware of goats."

With that, she walked away.

CHAPTER 3

*L*ayla left the Gryphon Avenue police station in a mood. She hated that Palmer had caught her helping herself at the jeweler's shop, and she really didn't appreciate him using that to wring her like a dishrag for information. Worse, it was her owned damned fault.

Her thoughts lingered over the interview as she made her way back to Hellion House. It was a half-hour walk from Gryphon Avenue if she took the alleyways, and it saved her the cost of a hackney. Not that she couldn't afford a cab, but she hung onto her coin out of habit. Or defiance. Just because she had money for the first time in her life, she wasn't about to spend it like a drunken sailor. No, she was a trollop, not a fool.

Except when it came to thievery, which was indeed forbidden by the mistress of Hellion House. She owed Mrs. Randall everything for saving her from the streets, but sometimes that burden was too much. Whether it made sense or not, breaking the rules gave her back the smallest crumb of control, and then she could breathe again for a while.

Maybe she was a fool, after all. Or mad. Palmer was a decent man, but he came from a far more orderly universe. At least, she thought he did. Unlike most men, Palmer didn't talk about himself or where he came from. All she knew was that sometimes he looked at her as if she might explode his tidy world to smithereens.

That thought finally made her smile.

Hellion House was on Maudlin Way, an old and threadbare part of the city crammed with ramshackle buildings. By comparison, the house was respectable, with fresh paint and all its trim in place. It even had a proper yard with old fruit trees—a definite luxury in a walled city where land was scarce.

The door swung open before she'd finished climbing the steps. It was Janey, with her wicked grin and messy fringe of fair hair. She was dressed in her aeronaut's leathers.

"She's waiting for you upstairs," Janey said without preamble. It went without saying she meant Mrs. Randall.

"Hello to you, too." Layla sailed past her friend. "Off to the airfield?"

"Testing an aether cannon." Janey shrugged. "Madam has asked me to look at it as a favor for a client."

"Anyone interesting?"

"One Mr. Bidwell."

"I don't know him," Layla said, her curiosity aroused.

"Neither do I, but he has an aether cannon."

"All men think that after a drink or two."

Janey shot her a dry look. "This one put his on a ship. A little more credible than most."

Layla laughed. "Let me know if it goes boom."

"That's more your department. Mine is to ensure it doesn't blow the ship to splinters."

With that, Janey left, boots thundering down the stairs. Layla stifled a pang of envy at the thought of riding an airship. Of having a trade the way Janey did as a pilot and a maker with a growing reputation. One day Janey would have a proper business with her name on the door—the missus would see to it. Keeping talent at her beck and call was simply good business.

Layla shut the door and turned the key in the lock. The click of iron reminded her of the police station and its uncomfortable little room. Despite herself, the thought made her shiver.

Turning on her heel, Layla went in search of Mrs. Randall, pausing long enough to shake the dust from her hems. The house was quiet, its inmates asleep or away on errands. The only sound was the soft strum of a guitar from the rooftop garden.

She found the proprietress of Hellion House in her office upstairs. The room was just large enough for a pair of burgundy wing-backed chairs and a large pecan writing desk with cabriole legs. Mrs. Randall sat behind it, her back to a narrow window shrouded in lace curtains.

The proprietress of Hellion House was somewhere in her mid-thirties, with lavish red hair and elven features. She was worldly, elegant, discreet, and, as far as Layla could tell, knew more about backroom politics than most of the Cabinet.

"Did you get the gallery case?" Mrs. Randall asked as soon as Layla approached the open door.

"I did, but Detective Inspector Palmer has it now."

Mrs. Randall looked up from the letter she was writing and carefully placed her pen in an ornate brass stand. "How very provoking. By what means did he get involved?"

Layla's stomach knotted. She suddenly felt like a girl again, wishing for the safety of her mother's skirts. Mrs. Randall had that effect, showing her displeasure without raising her voice or so much as flicking an eyelash. It just rose off her like frost.

"I'm sorry, ma'am. He saw me at Wordsworth's and guessed something was afoot."

Mrs. Randall folded her hands, as if praying for patience. "He would. He knows us too well."

He knows me too well. Layla controlled her features, pushing away all thoughts about the ring. "Then when he saw the case, he went serious, like he knew something. He seems to think it came from someplace outside Londria. A place he grew up in."

"Really?" Mrs. Randall's eyebrows rose. "How interesting."

"It touched a nerve all right. He asked a lot of questions."

"What did you tell him?"

"I told him what I knew. I had to explain why I'd bought it."

Mrs. Randall made a soft noise of displeasure. "Did he believe you?"

"Yes, eventually." Guilt dug its claws into Layla, making her long to squirm.

Mrs. Randall sat back, a sliver of sunshine gilding her upswept hair. "What's done can't be helped. What we do next is what matters. What you do next."

"They'll have the gallery case locked up," Layla said. "I can't just walk in and take it."

Mrs. Randall gestured to the closest chair, inviting her to sit. "Of course not. Besides, that would be a wasted opportunity. We want Palmer's abilities on our side."

"What for?" Layla gratefully sank into the soft seat. All that walking had left her with sore feet. "He's not one of us."

"We want to find the original owner of that case. So does he."

"So we let him keep it?"

"No, my dear." A smile brushed Mrs. Randall's lips. "We can't let this opportunity slip through our fingers. Finding out who ordered the destruction of the *Leopard* is only the first thread I mean to follow. Someone means to control Londria, perhaps all of Albion, and their reach is greater even than the mages once had. The more I learn, the faster I will understand this web of influence."

"What for?"

"To find the spider, of course. Perhaps to counteract its bite. Information is the one currency that never loses its value."

And Palmer had taken information from Layla with shameful

ease. Heat crept up the back of her neck. "Then what do you want me to do?"

Mrs. Randall tilted her head, considering. "You're very good at being my eyes and ears. The best operative I have. Besides, you're well able to look after yourself. Your escapades with the Anathema Club show that beyond a doubt."

A thrill ran through Layla's bones—part apprehension, part anticipation. "What exactly do you have in mind, ma'am?"

"If I know Palmer, he won't let this go. I need you to be part of his investigation, wherever it leads."

"I'm sorry, sir. We arrived at the Riverside Bazaar with all haste." Palmer clasped his hands behind his back, doing his best to look as sorry as he felt for his shortcomings.

It was the morning after the bloodbath, and he was in his captain's office. This was the after-action command performance. Palmer had been left standing, and the pattern of the carpet circled his feet like a bull's-eye.

"I know you did your best," Captain Sturgess replied, his thick mustache twitching with irritation. He paced to the window of his office and back again. "But Murray's wounds have given him a fever. Martindale was injured, too. He won't be using that arm for a month or more. Whitley ran and still hasn't been found. You are the last man standing, and so you are here to answer for the glory and the blame."

With that, Sturgess nudged the newspaper on top of his desk. Palmer read the upside-down headline: *Save our Citizens, or Save Police Salaries*. Palmer clamped his jaw tight, sure he'd regret anything he said. A childhood memory of having his knuckles caned floated up in his imagination.

"Have you anything to say?" Sturgess asked, rocking on his

heels. He resembled an agitated walrus in business attire. That didn't make Palmer any less wary. Walruses had deadly tusks.

"We contained and exterminated the threat, sir," Palmer replied. "All three subjects."

"But not before there were twice as many fatalities."

Palmer's temper slipped a degree. "Sir, we were fortunate there were not more deaths."

"I know." Sturgess paced a few steps, then turned back. "There was a body at the entrance to the bazaar."

Palmer nodded, the image of a dismembered leg rising up in his mind.

"That was the Lord Mayor's brother." Sturgess took a seat behind his desk and glowered up from a fortress of paperwork. "The good worthies of Londria are unamused. They expect respectable neighborhoods to be protected."

Palmer bridled. "The Unseen aren't unruly bullyboys we can haul in for a talking-to."

Sturgess slumped. "I know that, but logic doesn't matter. The gentlemen and ladies of the city have forgotten how happy they were to be rid of the Conclave and their rules. Now that there's nothing to keep the monsters away, they want us to fill that gap."

"We're not mages," Palmer replied. "Sir."

Captain Sturgess made a soft *harumph*. "They want blood, Palmer. They want someone's head to roll, and you survived when His Worship's brother did not. For your own sake, and the sake of the division, you would do well to vanish until public attention moves on to a fresh atrocity."

Palmer's jaw drifted open. "But we saved so many."

"And that matters." Sturgess looked away, studying the wall behind Palmer as if he'd never seen it before. "But they won't remember that for a week or two."

Vanishing meant not working, and that wasn't something Palmer could afford. "Sir, surely there are witness accounts that speak in our favor?"

"Of course there are. Unfortunately, chief among them is that of a fortune teller. A year ago, we—or more likely the mage's foot soldiers—would have arrested her for practicing unauthorized magic. Not exactly the friend we want. And then there's the matter of your working style. You're a brilliant detective who should be leading other brilliant detectives, and yet you always manage to find a way to work alone. You're exactly the type of officer the press loves to write about. They may romanticize a maverick, but they love to vilify loners even more."

Palmer inhaled to protest, but Sturgess held up a hand. "It's not just or fair, but some time away is completely practical. And, as I understand it, there is work that needs doing elsewhere."

"Sir? I don't understand."

"You should, given that you've already been involved in this case." As he spoke, Sturgess rose and crossed to the office door. He opened it and stood back, allowing new visitors to enter. "Mrs. Randall. Miss McHugh."

The two women entered, the bright colors of their garments startling amid the dull hues of the office. Mrs. Randall wore bottle green, Layla brilliant blue that set off her red-gold hair. He thought he'd seen Layla's every guise before—the coquette, the hunter, the maiden in distress. But today she looked softly respectable, with her hair in soft curls and pearl buttons from neck to wrist. She might have been an alderman's daughter, the kind of woman he would be assigned to protect. But she wasn't.

The blood began to pound in Palmer's ears. There was no version of events that made an alliance between Hellion House and his captain advisable. There was law, and then there was the murky chaos the women occupied. But Mrs. Randall had a way of making people—even a police captain—pay attention when it suited her.

Sturgess offered the women the two available guest chairs, then gave Palmer a narrow look. "I have heard from Mrs. Randall about the gallery case. That a client won it in a card game from one Mr. Polliver, who was involved with the destruction of the *Leopard*. And that same client sold the case to Wordsworth, the jeweler, and how it came to be in our evidence locker."

Words stuck in Palmer's throat. Something was up if Sturgess could gloss over Layla's visit to the station with the aplomb of a seasoned defense lawyer. "Very good, sir. If I may ask—"

Mrs. Randall broke in. "We're here because we need your help, Detective Inspector Palmer."

"Indeed, ma'am?" Palmer met her gaze.

She must have sensed his misgivings, because a faint flush crept along her cheekbones. "Yes. I had hoped that by acquiring and examining the gallery case, I might gather clues about Polliver's identity. Eventually discover who hired him."

"Why is that of concern to you?" Palmer asked. "Did you have a financial interest in the airship?"

He felt Layla's gaze on him with the heat of a physical touch. Concentration wavered until he forced it back under control.

"No, but a great many people died," Mrs. Randall said evenly. "I may be a private citizen and not an officer of law, but if I can play even a small part in bringing the saboteur to justice, I will consider it a victory."

And a piece of information you can use to your own ends. "We know it was the mages who ordered the destruction of the ship. Or their crazy band of admirers, the Threshers."

Mrs. Randall smiled up at him. "Or someone else who shared their interests. The devil, as they say, Mr. Palmer, is in the details. I would like to know who paid this Mr. Polliver, and who made the decision to do so."

Her tone chilled Palmer to the marrow. "You suspect something."

"The Conclave was brutal, as were their allies. That requires a certain mindset that does not disappear just because the evidence of its presence is swept away. It is like the underground tendrils of a mushroom patch awaiting rain so it can fruit again."

Her words hung in the air, silencing the others for a long moment. Her logic was sound, if hard to hear. He glanced at Sturgess, who nodded at Palmer to carry on.

"You say you need my help. What can I do for you?" he asked.

"Layla tells me that you recognize the origin of the case from its maker's mark."

If only he'd kept his mouth shut. "I do. It comes from Wilcolme Haven, an agricultural enclave to the northeast."

"How do you know that?" Layla asked, speaking for the first time since she sat down. Her chin had gone up, challenging him.

Palmer pulled a gold lighter from his jacket. When he flicked it open, a tiny clockwork dragon emerged with a whirr and puffed a miniature flame. "This came from the same workshop, which is in Wilcolme Haven."

"A fine piece," Mrs. Randall said.

"Thank you." He slid the lighter back into his pocket, finally breaking Layla's gaze. "Each piece from that workshop was custom-made. No other maker used the same mark."

He realized his mistake the moment the words were spoken. Mrs. Randall leaned forward, every line of her body intent. "If each piece is custom, then surely it should be possible to trace its history. Would you consider traveling to Wilcolme Haven to learn what you can about our Mr. Polliver—or whoever bought the case?"

Palmer froze. He'd sooner go to Hell. It had fewer complicated memories. Light-headed, he cast a desperate look toward his captain, but Sturgess had already laid the groundwork for his reply.

"Of course, ma'am," Sturgess replied. "My officers are here to serve."

"Is a journey absolutely necessary, sir?" Palmer replied, keeping his voice level by sheer willpower. "Perhaps correspondence would be more efficient?"

In fact, even with semi-regular airship access, communication with the havens was slow and unreliable. The captain's expression said as much.

"A journey is opportune, given recent events. It never hurts to look eager." Sturgess's subtext was clear. The citizens of Londria were hunting for a convenient scapegoat, and Palmer would do nicely. This was a good time to make himself scarce.

And Palmer needed his job. "Very good, sir."

CHAPTER 4

The Wayfarer was a Fletcher Industries aircraft shaped like two inflatable cigars harnessed in tandem and mounted by a schooner's-worth of sails. It was a medium-sized vessel, meant for carrying cargo and with enough fuel to make it to Wilcolme Haven and back at a brisk plod. The ship had slipped its mooring lines just after the mist was off the grass, and it was scheduled to arrive at Wilcolme around noon.

Palmer hated airships. Most saw them as gaily striped balloons, childlike in their brilliant silks. In truth, they were steam-powered death traps poised to ignite their highly combustible gas bags while sailing at gut-curdling heights. Reasonable people wouldn't climb aboard, but he had his orders, so here he was.

And here Layla was, one more factor to worry about. She had no business being on the ship, and even less traveling to the bumcrack of beyond, but Mrs. Randall had insisted and backed up her insistence by paying for the flight. Of course, Sturgess had agreed, the police budget being what it was. If the proprietress of Hellion House wanted her eyes and ears on the investigation, why would a mere police captain object? Which left Palmer exactly no room to complain.

"Have you flown on an airship before?" Layla asked, raising her voice above the beat of the propellers and the hum of wind through the many ropes and lines. She was wrapped in a heavy shawl and a quilted violet pelisse trimmed with heavy braid. A long scarf secured her hat and tied under her chin, the ends fluttering in the sharp breeze. By her ebullient smile, she was having the time of her life. "You must have taken a flight when you came to Londria."

"Of course," Palmer replied, glad he was wearing gloves. They hid the fact he was gripping the rail hard enough that his knuckles must be turning white. "That was years ago."

A dozen years, in fact. Time had passed in that strange, elastic way that seemed both decades and minutes long. Hadn't he just boarded the airship for Londria, seventeen and praying that he'd done enough to secure his brother's future? What would he find in Wilcolme once they docked? Would Kieran even want to see him after all this time?

Palmer and Layla stood together at the side of the ship, keeping out of the way of the crew. *The Wayfarer* made regular monthly supply runs to the agricultural enclaves, but took few passengers and offered even fewer creature comforts. That didn't seem to bother Layla, who barely seemed to notice the bob and sway of the airship.

"You haven't traveled since you came to the city?" she asked.

"Holidays are a rich man's pleasure."

She nodded with a rueful look of understanding. "And I suppose you don't chase many thieves into the air."

"They head for the port. It's easier to hide on a proper ship."

"But the scenery is not as pretty."

He had to agree to that much, anyway. The Outlands—the wilderness beyond the walled cities—stretched below, sunlight playing over the dense greenery and ribbons of blue-green water. The landscape was beautiful, but all that green hid the monsters in its shadows. Unseen were the deadliest predators, but they weren't the only ones.

Movement caught his attention as one of the airmen climbed up the rigging like a spider, doing something to a device strapped to a spar. Another airman bellowed an order, and a canvas sheet unfurled and bellied with wind. Palmer felt the tug of added propulsion beneath his feet and instinctively reached for Layla, but she remained steady, her blue eyes bright with interest at everything around her.

No, she shouldn't have been there. Palmer had fled Wilcolme Haven for a reason. It was a violent, dirty, lawless hole. The first order of business would be to leave Layla somewhere safe while he did what needed doing. That was his best way of protecting her. Then they'd catch the first flight out.

"This is my first time out of Londria," Layla announced, almost breathless with wonder. "Is it all like this? The Outlands, I mean. It looks so wild."

"Not all of it." It wasn't her fault she didn't know enough to be terrified.

"There are the havens, correct? Like the one we're going to?" She looked suddenly sheepish. "I'm sorry to ask, but what's in the havens?"

Typical city girl, who never thought to ask where the oats for her porridge came from. "Farms. Mines. Mills. They're all different. There's not enough room in the city for everything, and so the havens exist to send food and supplies into the urban areas."

"What's it like living in one?" she asked, tilting her head as she studied his face.

Deadly. Desperate. He thought about telling the truth, but silence was a habit. "Wilcolme is bigger than some. It has its own mage."

Mages tended the magical wards that kept the Unseen outside

the perimeter of the settlement. Otherwise, anything with a heartbeat would be dead and eaten in a single night.

"The haven's mage wouldn't have fallen along with the Citadel?" she asked.

"No. The Citadel protected Londria, not the Outlands, and not the other cities." And someday, Palmer was sure those surviving mages would make the rebellious Londrians pay—but that was tomorrow's problem. Today, his dance card was full.

He checked his pocket watch, which showed fifteen minutes had passed since he last looked. After two hours in the air, he desperately wanted a cigarette, but open flames were strongly discouraged so close to flammable gasses. He put the watch away and glared at the treetops.

"Do you still have friends in Wilcolme?" Layla asked.

He flinched, but he didn't let it reach his face. His private life wasn't up for discussion. "I don't know who is left there."

"Really?"

He rounded on her, his temper piqued by so many questions, but he checked himself. His anger would betray the lie, and that was none of her business, either. "Life is hard there. People don't stay long, not if they have any chance to leave. This journey is most likely a fool's errand."

She narrowed her eyes slightly, as if bringing him into focus. Palmer turned away. The women in her profession were expert at reading their clients. Ironically, that skill was one thing they had in common with the police.

The ship banked, pulling him out of his thoughts. The carpet of trees fell away, revealing fieldstone walls surrounding a patchy cluster of fields. Herds of sheep and stocky cows dotted the emerald grass. With a sudden, sickening jolt, he knew exactly where he was—just south of their destination. Layla crowded next to him, pulling her shawl close. The ship tilted, bringing the soft press of her side against his as she gazed with rapt wonder at the rolling waves of wheat.

"I've never seen anything like it," Layla said in wonder. "So much open space."

That was true. There was room to move here, room to run and play. To explore in ways no city child could imagine. There was also no place to hide if the Unseen got past the wards. It was one of the first life lessons he could remember.

"What's it like to live in a place like this?" she asked.

"The world looks very different. The havens raise food for a magical, luxurious city none of the workers ever visit."

"What's that?" she pointed to a stone tower that spanned the winding river.

"The wheelhouse," he replied, remembering climbing the tower as a boy, always in a race with his brother. "It runs the mill. The River Rats trade up and down the waters, and they came to Wilcolme for the flour. Sometimes they bought fleece in shearing season. They weren't allowed into the town, but they'd come to the dock and set up a tent to do business. It was like a holiday. Everyone would go to see what they had to sell."

She gave a soft laugh. "You almost smiled right then. You should do it more often."

Palmer stiffened, but there was no chance to retort. An airman marched toward them, sporting bars beneath the golden arrow insignia of Fletcher Industries. That made him the senior crew hand, second only to the captain on a ship of this size.

"Please take a seat inside the cabin and prepare for landing." The man spread his arms as if they were geese he meant to herd off the road.

"Is the airfield still beside the north gate?" Palmer asked.

The airman shook his head. "Closer in now. Barely a five-minute walk to the town center. I think His Worship likes to see who comes and goes."

A trickle of cold ran down Palmer's spine. According to the records back at Gryphon Avenue, Mayor Ryerson had passed on, but there was no record of who ran the Haven now. But he'd find out soon enough. With luck, the place would be filled with new faces. He had no desire to reminisce.

Palmer and Layla took their seats in the cabin with a handful of other passengers. Under the watchful eye of the crew, they grabbed the worn leather straps dangling from the ceiling as handholds and endured the lurching ride to the ground. They weren't allowed to stand again until the broad gondola of the airship was firmly tethered down.

"Passengers out!" cried the senior crew hand. "Have your papers ready!"

Palmer held the cabin door for Layla. "Our first stop will be the Wisteria Inn. It's the only place with rooms to rent, so don't expect much."

She touched his arm lightly. "We both know I'm a good survivor."

With that, she sailed across the deck and down the gangplank to the field below. Palmer followed, taking in glimpses of the town through the crowd of workers gathering to haul cargo away. Some rooflines looked familiar, others new. Palmer tried to stem the flood of memories crashing in like an angry surf, but it was all he could do to keep his professional mask in place.

A few yards ahead, officers of the Watch waited to inspect the new arrivals. Sweat trickled down the back of his neck.

"The watchmen have rifles, but everyone else has crossbows," Layla observed in a low voice. "Isn't that a bit primitive?"

"Rifles are expensive," Palmer replied. "Arrows or bolts can be made locally. We all learn to shoot as soon as we can walk."

Endless practice with the short, recurved weapons that burned itself into muscle and bone. Just the sight of the bows, and the gears and wheels that quickly managed the heavy draw, kindled the feel of the fletching between his fingers. He shook off the clinging sensation, hating the associations it revived.

Palmer and Layla were at the back of the line. He strained to see the watchmen's faces, wondering if any were the same officers who'd chased his younger self after this prank or that. But while the green and black uniforms were familiar, the men wearing them were not. The tension in his gut released a notch.

A raucous bleat caught his attention. Someone nearby had a herd of goats, and it looked as if they'd escaped their pen. A black-and-white buck with curving horns paraded past the edge of the crowd. It paused to sniff the crates being offloaded from the ship.

The line shuffled ahead. It was Layla's turn. Palmer had been carrying her valise, but surrendered it so that she could go ahead. As she moved forward, she summoned her brilliant smile, all but blinding the flustered watchman. Palmer frowned at the spectacle until his turn came.

"Papers," demanded the watchman.

Palmer offered his identity card and police credentials.

The officer studied them without interest until he consulted the list on his clipboard. Then his brows angled down. "Stop where you are, sir."

Palmer froze as two more watchmen flanked the first. Layla stood with the crowd on the other side of the checkpoint, looking back with gathering dismay. She recognized the tone in the watchman's voice—the one that said the game was up and the handcuffs were out.

Old instincts reared up, flooding Palmer's blood with the urge to fight or bolt. It was the place, the pungent smell of the farming town and the way the light played off the weathered boards of the houses. The knowledge that death lay just beyond the trees, and there was nothing to fill the time between now and then but mindless toil.

He refused to be trapped there again.

The watchman stepped forward. "Liam Alexander Palmer, you are under arrest for the murder of Samuel Babbington."

Time slowed, the words slurring to a meaningless drone.

Alarm flared in Palmer's chest, a lightning flash of rage and denial. He heard Layla's outraged cry, but didn't look up.

When the watchmen paused to draw breath, Palmer made his choice. He bolted, breaking for the open field. He'd made it out of there once. He could do it again.

He was moving too fast to stop when he collided with the goat.

CHAPTER 5

The bawling bleat of the outraged goat made every head turn. Layla stared open-mouthed as Palmer bounced off the animal, landing on one knee. The goat skittered backward, lowering its horned head to charge. Palmer scrambled to rise, but the watchmen pounced first, dragging the detective to his feet.

Layla's stomach plunged, the valise she carried slipping from her fingers to land in the dust at her feet. She'd imagined problems with this trip—illness, delays, bad food, turbulence—but not this. She had been counting on Palmer to navigate this place. He was nothing if not reliable.

And yet there he was, shoulders hunched and head down as three watchmen marched him away in cuffs. He'd struggled, but it had been cut short when the head watchmen had drawn a pistol. Apparently, the bully boys in charge could afford something besides the strange clockwork bows.

Layla watched in stunned amazement as the watchmen loaded Palmer onto a mule-drawn cart, no doubt to take him to wherever prisoners were held. Blood oozed from a scrape on his cheekbone where he'd hit the ground. Then his pale face vanished as they thrust a sack over his head.

By the satisfaction on his captor's faces, someone was getting a bonus for this arrest. Why? What was Palmer's story?

The crowd fell into a cowed silence, as if they weren't sure what had just happened. With an angry flip of its tail, the goat bounded away.

The driver whipped up the mule. The grind of iron wheels on gravel sounded like giant teeth crunching bones. Layla snatched up her valise, casting a glance around her. She was alone in this forsaken place, but at least no one was taking an unwelcome interest in her presence. The best play was to keep moving until she could make a plan.

She kept her pace unhurried as she left the airfield and turned toward what passed for the town. At first glance, it was small, no bigger than the clutch of houses that sprang up around one of Londria's many factories. There were few trees, leaving the afternoon sun to blaze down with an uncompromising glare. What greenery there was ran in a broad stripe next to the river, where she glimpsed a clutch of rowboats pulled up alongside a wooden dock.

Palmer's story about the River Rats played in her mind for a moment. She'd always guessed by his accent that he'd come from outside Londria, but had thought it someplace nicer than this. Had he been one of those boys with more swagger than pennies, pretending he was too old to want the toys and sweets on offer?

Like he was too good to want her? The way he'd hauled her into the station still stung, but she let the thought go. They had bigger problems than her wounded pride.

She'd reached the town proper now. The buildings were wind-worn and patched together, their colors filtered through a haze of dust. The tallest might have boasted three stories behind its false front, and none had the rooftop gardens Layla was used to seeing in the city. In a single word, Wilcolme Haven was shabby. And yet, there was an airfield and a town watch with proper uniforms. Someone here had money.

Oddly, that gave her a shred of confidence. Her profession relied on picking out the richest mark in the room, and then unwrapping their vices with a connoisseur's touch. Her interest, first and always, was gathering information. The difference now was her goal. All at once, Polliver was a secondary concern. She had to get herself—and Palmer—out of this place.

Layla's feet echoed on the boardwalk that ran beside the dirt road through town. Uneasiness crept over her, clinging like the grit borne by the wind. There was something wrong about the buildings besides their neglected state, and it took her another minute to figure out what it was. They were blind, the windows filled in or never there at all. She'd seen this in a few places close to the city wall, where the homes were boarded up against the Unseen. Despite the heat, her skin went clammy.

Layla quickened her step and then stopped, aware that she was already panting. It was unseasonably hot, at least a dozen degrees warmer than in Londria. The breeze smelled of animals and wood smoke—and, unexpectedly, pie. The sweet scent of pastry wafted from a larger building to her left. A sign nailed above the front door proclaimed it was the Wisteria Inn, although the only vegetation in sight was a weed sprouting through cracks in the foundation wall.

The place wasn't much, but Palmer had said there was only one hotel. If she wanted a roof tonight, this was it.

Layla entered, noting the faded wallpaper and well-trodden carpet runner. A desk sat inside the front door, and on top was a thick, heavy ledger, presumably a register of guests. She glanced around and, finding herself alone, scanned the last several pages of untidy scrawl. Unfortunately, most of the names were illegible and, as far as she could determine, none were Polliver. She returned the book to its original position.

She rang the brass bell screwed to the desktop. The sound

startled a rangy cat from the shadows, sending it up the stairs in an orange streak. A moment later, Layla heard the click of heels approaching from the back of the house.

A stocky female in an apron pushed through the door at the back of the entry hall and approached in a cloud of warm, cinnamon-scented air. The woman's square face was flushed, presumably with heat from a stove, although Layla also caught a whiff of spirits. Gin, perhaps.

"First time in Wilcolme?" the woman asked by way of greeting. Her accent was like Palmer's, the vowels just a shade longer than a Londrian's might be. A muslin cap sat atop her cloud of frizzy gray hair. She might have looked grandmotherly, except for her calculating gaze.

"Yes," Layla replied. "I need a room."

"For how long?" The woman opened the register to a fresh page.

"I'm not sure yet. A week to start." Layla fervently hoped to be long gone by then, but instinct said to keep her plans to herself.

"Money's due in advance." The woman put a hand on her hip.

Layla paid and signed the register in a florid scrawl as unreadable as the rest. By the way the woman watched as Layla pulled out her purse, she was glad the bulk of her funds were hidden out of sight. Better not to appear worth robbing.

"They call me Mrs. Bethany," the woman announced. "Breakfast is at seven o'clock sharp. Dinner is at eight. Guests find their own tea. I tell the ladies to stay away from the tavern, but there aren't many options."

"Thank you," Layla replied with her best smile. "Are those the only places folks gather?"

The landlady studied her, then waved a hand toward the staircase. "Pretty much. I'll show you to your room."

Layla picked up her bag and followed. The doors on the next floor were numbered along a hallway that ended in a smaller stairway to the third floor. She was in room number five. It was adequate, if small, with a wardrobe, bed, and washstand. The nicest thing in it was a cross-stitched sampler proclaiming *We Welcome You Our Lovely Guest*.

"I didn't make that," Mrs. Bethany said when she saw Layla admiring the needlework. "That was the former owner. She passed away some years back."

"Do you get many guests?"

"Just enough to keep the doors open. That said, there are a few rules to follow in this house."

Layla set down her bag. "Which are?"

"No pets, no visitors." She studied Layla with sharp interest. "What business do you have in town?"

"I'm looking for opportunities," Layla replied. It was a line she'd used before, vague enough to fit a host of situations.

"There are only so many reasons a pretty woman arrives alone in a place like Wilcolme Haven." The landlady raised her eyebrows. "Most of them spell a woman in trouble. I'd say that was you."

Layla flinched inside. "You mistake me. I'm not in any trouble."

"Then you *are* the trouble," Mrs. Bethany said evenly. "I run an honest establishment, mind. I have a reputation to keep pure."

This was a game. The airfield goat was purer than this old baggage. "I'm sure you do."

"I hope you understand my position."

Layla reminded herself this was the only place with rooms for rent. "I trust you can introduce me to the right people. Those people you know who would appreciate trouble."

"I could do that."

"For a consideration."

A slow smile creased the woman's face. "I'm glad we understand one another."

Layla carefully removed her hat and smoothed a stray lock of hair back into place. This wasn't how she'd intended to gather information, but she could work with it. "Tell me all about this opportunity. What is his name?"

∼

Layla left the Wisteria Inn some time later. More people were about now that the sun had peaked and the air was cooler. Like the blind buildings, the haven's citizens seemed faded. The only merriment came from a pack of children frolicking on a patch of trampled grass while a figure in mage's robes led them in a singsong rhyme. This must be the mage who powered the haven's wards against the Unseen. She paused to watch a moment, her toes wanting to tap along with the rhythm of the chant. All the mages she'd ever seen were the grim, frightening officials of Londria's Conclave. Good to know that Wilcolme Haven held at least one pleasant surprise.

She eventually found the low wooden building that housed the haven's jail. She'd debated the wisdom of admitting that she knew a hunted fugitive, but a visit was the fastest way to learn the details of his arrest. And speed was a virtue well worth the notoriety of Palmer's acquaintance. She'd only been in Wilcolme Haven a few hours, and the place already made her anxious.

She presented herself at the front office, where one of the watchmen from the airfield lounged with eyes shut and his boots on the desk. Clearly, his superior wasn't around. She gave a polite cough, and he scrambled to his feet.

"Ma'am?" The young man smoothed back his thick brown hair and tugged his jacket straight. He was gangly, as if he hadn't yet grown into his limbs.

Young was good. Youngsters were easy to impress. This one still had spots on his chin.

"I'm here to see one of your prisoners. His name is Palmer." Layla gave a wavering smile, as if the expression took the last of her courage. "Mrs. Bethany gave me directions to this place."

The watchman's look grew wary at the mention of the landlady. "Did she now? And may I be so bold as to ask your name, ma'am?"

Layla let the question hang in the air as she studied the bare brick walls and plain wooden desks. The only attempt at decor was a faded portrait of the queen beside the door to the back office, which presumably belonged to the watch's absent commanding officer. It was as far from Hellion House as Layla could imagine.

"Miss McHugh," she finally said.

The watchman stooped to make a note of the name in a black-bound book that sat open on the desk. "There's nothing in my orders about the prisoner receiving visitors."

"Is there anything in your orders forbidding it?" She tried the watery smile again, but he looked doubtful as he set down his pencil.

"Don't waste your time, miss. He's a bad one. No one ever thought to see him again, and good riddance, by all accounts."

That didn't sound at all like Palmer. "What was his crime?"

The watchman's mouth pulled flat. "Murder."

Surprise ran down Layla's spine in a cold shiver. "Murder? Are you certain?"

"I am." He pointed to a sketch pinned to the wall. It did resemble a younger version of the Palmer she knew, thinner and with a feral look about the eyes.

Layla heaved an impatient sigh. "He's a detective inspector in the Londria police force. How is it possible that he rose through the ranks if he's under suspicion of a terrible crime?"

The watchman shrugged. "Mail gets lost in the Outlands."

She pondered that for a moment. True, news could be slow to reach the haven It was far more likely that this accusation was utter nonsense. "I would like to see him, please, Officer..."

"Sanderson," he supplied. "You say Mrs. Bethany sent you around?"

"Indeed, she did." Interesting that he'd circled back to that particular point. "She promised that I would get to make my farewells to Mr. Palmer."

"Did she?" he said with no enthusiasm.

"Yes," she said, pressing a hand to her heart in a gesture of unspoken sorrow. "There are things—delicate things—I would not wish to leave unsaid."

In truth, she wanted to scream at Palmer that he was an addle-brained ninny to come near this circle of hell, and a greater fool for bringing her along. Nonetheless, she did her best to look forlorn. It was all in the pout and trembling chin.

Finally, Officer Sanderson weakened, reaching for the bundle of keys at his belt. "All right then, but make it quick."

She followed him down a narrow hall to the back of the building. There were three cells with small, barred windows high up in their heavy wooden doors. Each was fixed with an iron lock the size of Layla's fist, but two of the doors stood open. Sanderson stopped at the third and inserted a large black key. The lock turned with a grinding sound that set Layla's teeth on edge.

When the door swung open, she saw Palmer slumped on a plain wooden bench, his head in his hands. He didn't look up.

"Please, may we have some privacy?" she asked the watchman.

"You've got fifteen minutes," Sanderson replied.

Layla stepped inside and winced as the door thumped closed behind her. She remained silent until she heard the man's steps fade away, then turned to Palmer. An unexpected surge of anger brought heat to her cheeks.

"What the bloody hell is going on?" she demanded in a low voice.

He lifted his head and returned her glare. "What are you doing here?"

She took a step closer, doing her best to loom over Palmer. It was hard to do when wearing such a fashionable shade of violet.

"I came here to do a job, and I can't do it if you're locked in here."

He looked away, as if fascinated by the opposite wall. "Then don't. Get back on the first airship leaving this place."

"Why didn't you tell me you were wanted for murder?"

He jammed his fingers through his fair hair. "I had no idea."

The words held an edge of panic that prickled the back of Layla's neck and underscored their strange reversal. In a sane world, she would be the one under lock and key and he would be the one asking questions. Anger forgotten, she sat next to him on the battered wooden bench, grateful she had enough petticoats to guard against slivers. "What happened when you left the first time?"

"That was a dozen years ago. I got on an airship and sailed away."

"That's all?"

He closed his eyes as if infinitely weary. "I was seventeen. I'd saved just enough coin to get out of this place."

"How did your family feel about that?"

"They had no opinion. My brother and I were charity boarders at the school."

Orphans, in other words. "You were young to be on your own."

"Nothing new in a place like this." His mocking tone said it all. "All it takes is for the wards to fail for a minute or two."

"Is that what happened?"

He nodded. "One day I had parents, and the next Kieran and I were on our own."

Unseen. It took Layla a moment to find her voice. "What became of your brother?"

"He was fourteen when I left, just old enough for an apprenticeship. I got him a place with Marvelle, the clockmaker. That was the best I could do to look after him." His mouth twisted, as if he'd tasted something foul. Guilt, perhaps?

"Do you regret that?"

"No," he said with finality, and then folded his arms. "Kieran loved the work, but I had none of his ability. I needed to do something else, so I left."

"Did you mean to come back?"

He gave his head a slight shake. "I was going to send for him when I had the money."

"But making your way in Londria without kin or connection wasn't easy."

Palmer shook his head again.

Layla knew what it was like to be on her own far too young. She would have thought it impossible, but she and Palmer had common ground. "So where does the murder come in? Who do they say you killed?"

His face tensed, as if he strained to keep memories at bay. "Sam Babbington, the schoolmaster. I don't know who accused me, and I don't know why."

"How was he killed?"

"Stabbed." The word was nearly a growl. "Listen. You can't help me, but you can finish what we came here to do. I mentioned a clockmaker named Marvelle. It's his mark on the gallery case. Go talk to him, see what you can find out, and then get back to Londria as soon as you can. If I am convicted of this murder, it does you no good to be here." His expression grew intense, as if he willed her to mark every word.

Layla dropped her gaze, suddenly needing the privacy of her thoughts. "I'm not leaving you here."

He gave a derisive huff. "You don't have a choice."

Layla forced herself to meet his dark-brown gaze. "Maybe I can prove you're innocent."

"How?"

"Is there no one who could give you an alibi?"

His expression grew opaque, as if a wall had come up around his soul. The sudden distance between them, or maybe the danger in the air, made her yearn to touch him. In a fairy tale, sometimes human touch could break an evil spell. But that was fiction, and she kept her hands folded on her lap.

"People in the havens don't dwell in the past," he said, his voice flat. "Half will be dead and the rest will have forgotten the details."

"What about your brother?"

Anger flashed. There and gone in an instant. "He doesn't know anything. He was with the seamstress when it happened. Marvelle ordered him new clothes."

Layla filed that tidbit away, along with Palmer's flash of temper. He was still the protective older brother. "Very well, but I'll still ask around. It might take me a day or two."

"My trial—or what passes for one in the havens—will happen in three days. The sentence won't be incarceration. Wilcolme doesn't have the resources to keep prisoners for long."

Layla felt the blood drain from her face. "The gallows?"

Palmer's laugh was harsh. "The havens banish the guilty to the forest. The Unseen are happy to accept our exiles."

CHAPTER 6

Palmer couldn't quite read the expression that passed over Layla's face. It might have been anger, or pity, or both. She caught his shoulder in one gloved hand and leaned close. At first he thought she'd whisper something the guard should not hear, but instead her soft lips brushed his cheek.

He drew back, a sudden lurch in his chest. "What was that for?"

"Courage." She rose in a rustle of skirts. "You're not alone."

Loneliness didn't bother him. It was a state he'd grown used to in the great, smoky city of Londria. It seemed the more people there were, the less one individual mattered. He'd seen that time and again on the job.

Still, Palmer's attention was inexorably dragged to the perfect fullness of her mouth. She'd smelled like berries warm from the sun. He wanted more, but a doomed man had no right to ask. Or maybe he'd been alone so long he couldn't remember the right words.

But then he thought of something he could ask. Something safe. "If you see Kieran at Marvelle's workshop, don't tell him I'm here."

"Don't you want to see him?" she asked.

He tried to imagine meeting his brother again. What he would say. What Kieran would say. The thoughts slid away like darting fish. "I want to keep him as far away from this as I can."

"What if he wants to see you?"

"Let him think I got away from this place. He'll learn the truth soon enough. But if you can, send me word of how he fares."

The corners of her mouth jerked down, but she gave a silent nod. Then footfalls approached the cell, accompanied by the clink of keys. Layla turned to face the door, her shoulders squared. When it opened, she walked out without a backward glance. The door slammed again, leaving Palmer alone. Only then did he realize she'd spared him the ritual of goodbyes.

He slumped forward on the bench, elbows resting on his knees. What light there had been had faded to gray, stealing the little color there was. The skitter of insects sent a prickle down his spine.

He craved a cigarette, but they'd taken all his smoking supplies. The only thing they hadn't managed to take away were his twisting thoughts.

Samuel Babbington. He'd taken them in when Palmer was barely old enough to tie his own shoes. Some named Babbington a charitable saint, and maybe he was by the haven's standards. The boys were mouths to feed in a place that survived by sheer willpower. And yet he'd fed and clothed them, and given them a sound education. Good enough that years later, Palmer had sailed through the police academy with top honors.

But once the school was shut for the day, they became chore boys who hauled water and chopped wood until their hands bled. It wasn't that Babbington had been a harsh taskmaster, but that he had enjoyed the sensation of control. The boys slept in an unfinished attic that let in the snow and rain while Babbington enjoyed a cozy bed. Babbington revered the willow switch. He would leave one of his charges out in a killing storm or forget to feed them or whatever random cruelty suited his fancy. For a long time, Palmer simply endured and focused on survival.

But not Kieran. Palmer tried to protect his brother, but there was only so much a boy could do against the adult world.

His brother had been slow to speak, and then slower to read. He learned with his hands and haunted Marvelle's workshop as soon as he could see over the edge of the workbench. But he was hopeless at schoolwork—and everything else Babbington asked of him. Kieran suffered the bite of the switch night after night after night. Afterward, he would sit and rock, holding his head in his hands, mute with defiance. Eventually, he stopped speaking altogether.

The lock rattled again, wrenching Palmer from his memories. The cell had gone completely dark, and he winced as the jailor's lantern blinded him.

"Here's your supper." Officer Sanderson set a tray with a cup and bowl inside the door and pushed it forward with one booted toe. Murky liquid slopped over the rim of the bowl.

"Tell me," Palmer said, still caught in the web of his memories. "How is old Marvelle?"

The watchman paused before replying. "He died years ago."

"But what about—"

Sanderson left before Palmer could finish the question. *What about my brother?*

Palmer stared down at the supper the young man had left. Fortunately, the tidal wave of watery stew hadn't doused the short stub of the candle stuck to the tray. It cast a flickering light over the cell, making monsters in the shadows.

If Marvelle was dead, was Kieran still at the workshop? Did he make the gallery case for Polliver? If not Kieran, then who? And word had it that Polliver was here. Why? Was he here to tie off loose ends?

A knot of anxiety lodged in Palmer's throat, making it hard to breathe. Layla was determined to do what she could to help him.

He touched the cheek she had kissed, then snatched his hand away. He should have insisted she leave. He couldn't protect her.

Just like he'd never been able to protect his little brother.

The candle guttered out.

～

AFTER NIGHTFALL, Layla accompanied Mrs. Bethany across the patch of dust and gravel that passed for the town square. It was easy to find their way. The half moon hung close and indecently bright in the indigo sky, with few lights to dim its shine. In contrast, shadows flooded in from the sky and the forest, pressing in on the scatter of houses like a rushing wave.

Layla missed the tall, protective weight of Londria's stone buildings. The haven had nothing over three stories, making the moon and stars feel close enough to whisper in her ear. She didn't like the sense of being exposed, especially as the light disappeared. The eyeless houses hinted at dangers in the dark.

They mounted the wooden steps of the town's largest residence, their boot heels echoing on the boards. It was not an elegant house, but it had three stories and was recently painted. Mrs. Bethany had said little about the excursion, beyond a recommendation for Layla to look her best. Layla hadn't packed evening wear—she was there to investigate, not attend a ball—and had to make do with her burgundy afternoon dress.

"Did you say the mayor lives here?" she asked as Mrs. Bethany reached for the door knocker.

"Hardwin." The landlady's smile was brief. She'd transformed from a flour-dusted innkeeper to a matron of consequence. The ribbed silk of her dress was the most luxurious thing Layla had yet seen in the town. "He'll make it worthwhile for both of us if he likes you."

Layla nodded her assent. Befriending the most powerful individual in the room was standard protocol for anyone in her profession, and especially useful now. The mayor was in the best position to set Palmer free. If he could tell her something about Polliver, so much the better.

There was the sound of several locks turning, and the door swung open to reveal a servant girl of about fourteen, who immediately curtsied at the sight of Mrs. Bethany. "Welcome, ma'am," she said in a small, anxious voice. "His Worship is in the library with the other guests."

They left their wraps with the girl and made their way into the house, Layla trailing a step behind Mrs. Bethany as she studied their surroundings. From the inside, she could see there were indeed a series of deadbolts securing the front door. The entrance hall had dark wainscoting that persisted as they passed room after room down a long and badly-lit corridor. Each chamber was large but badly furnished, with too many stuffed animal heads and not enough cushions on the horsehair seats. There were a few costly objects—a small but exquisite painting here, a silver candlestick there—but their styles were disjointed, as if they'd come from different collections. The only nod to a woman's touch was a spinning wheel coated in a thin film of dust. Was there no Mrs. Hardwin, then?

As they entered the spacious library, conversation paused. For a room supposedly dedicated to books, there was only one floor-to-ceiling bookcase. Instead, two card tables and several groupings of chairs filled the space. There were six couples and a smattering of single men, most with drinks in their hands, and more guests were still trickling in. They were dressed in styles from a few years ago, but all had made an effort at polish. Even so, there was a hardness to their faces, as if only fighters survived in the havens. Layla put on her best smile—the one that was radiant and just a touch flirtatious. Almost all the men smiled back, while the women did not. If Layla had to guess, she was not the first woman Mrs. Bethany had introduced to the haven. What had become of the others?

The tallest man stepped forward, his arms wide in a gesture of welcome. "Olive, how pleasant to see you. And you brought us some fresh blood to enliven our evening."

Mrs. Bethany's face pinked as she allowed their host to kiss her cheek. "Allow me to introduce Miss McHugh. I'm sure you shall enjoy getting to know one another."

He turned to Layla and grasped her gloved hand between both of his. "Enchanted. I'm Roderick Hardwin, the Mayor of Wilcolme Haven. Welcome to our little town."

So, this was the man Layla was supposed to please. He was somewhere in his late forties, with a workman's solid frame beneath a gentleman's suit. He was handsome enough, with dark hair and a closely-trimmed beard that couldn't hide wind-weathered skin. Whoever Hardwin was, he'd done well for himself.

Layla summoned all her charm, allowing him to keep holding her hand. "Delighted to make your acquaintance, Mayor Hardwin."

His bright blue eyes skimmed her from head to toe. Calculation flashed across his face, reminding Layla of a horse dealer about to make a shrewd bargain.

"Do I meet with your approval?" she asked in a quiet voice. He might bargain, but so could she.

Mrs. Bethany sucked in her breath, but Hardwin merely nodded. "You're a bold one, aren't you?"

"I like plain speaking when it serves a purpose, and you're clearly a confident man. If we dance, let it be with something besides words."

Hardwin smiled, revealing a chipped front tooth. One hand stroked the gold watch chain shimmering against his waistcoat. "Oh, indeed, I look forward to it. However, I see some new faces have arrived. Allow me to dispense with niceties so that we can have a proper chat."

"That suits me to perfection."

The mayor gave a slight nod. "My dear Mrs. Bethany, would

you be so kind as to introduce Miss McHugh to my other guests?"

The landlady took Layla's elbow and steered her across the room. "Well done. He likes you."

Layla didn't reply. Any novice at Hellion House could have managed the introduction. Finding out what hid behind Hardwin's smooth confidence would take more skill. Thus far, she'd only seen two servants. A man with few servants and many locks had something to hide.

"Have a care of Mrs. Cartwright," Mrs. Bethany whispered. "She's the mayor's regular mistress."

Layla caught sight of a slender woman in periwinkle blue, who returned Layla's glance with narrowed eyes. She was only a year or two older than Layla, but discontent dragged at her features.

"Her?" Layla asked under her breath. "She looks too ill-tempered to inspire carnal thoughts."

"She's done well enough for herself." Mrs. Bethany nodded to a brawny man at one of the tables. "That's her husband playing cards. He's the town butcher. The couple by the window are the teacher and his wife."

She looked around, curious because of Palmer's story. This teacher had replaced the man Palmer had supposedly murdered. "I saw some children playing earlier today. Are there many young ones here?"

Mrs. Bethany gave a slight shrug. "Enough grow up to keep the farms running."

Layla's step hitched as she imagined children working so close to the forest. A moment of curious play might take them beneath the trees and then—Layla forced her mind away from the image and accepted a drink from the single manservant taking care of the guests.

"And is that the mage?" Layla asked, nodding toward the tall, robed figure she'd seen earlier that afternoon.

Mrs. Bethany rolled her eyes skyward. "Yes. He and the mayor get along like two magnets repelling one another."

As the teacher's wife pulled Mrs. Bethany into conversation, Layla surveyed the room. More people had arrived, filling the generous space. Judging by the size of the town, anyone who mattered must be here.

Layla's attention returned to the mage, who leaned against the wall with a goblet in his hand. Normally one could tell the rank of a mage by the shade of his robes—darkest for the most junior and growing lighter as they rose up the ranks. These robes were so faded, it was hard to tell what color they'd once been. The man himself looked just as rumpled, his gray hair unruly and lines of fatigue bracketing his mouth. Intrigued, she crossed the room to introduce herself. A forward move for a female in polite circles, but she didn't think Wilcolme Haven stood on ceremony.

He straightened as she approached. He was a bear of a man, well over six feet tall and broad through the shoulders. His eyes were a pale gray that missed nothing.

"I do not remember you," he said as Layla drew up before him. "Surely that is an unforgivable oversight."

"Miss McHugh." She extended a hand. "I just arrived in the haven today, so no oversight occurred."

He squeezed her hand warmly. "Mage Bentley. If I may ask, my dear, why are you here? Only the desperate venture this far afield."

"I came with a friend," she said.

"Liam Palmer," he replied.

"Yes." Her interest in the mage sharpened. "Do you know him?"

"I did. He was foolishly optimistic, like most children." The mage took a swallow of his wine. "They believe things should be fair at that age."

Layla tried to imagine Palmer as an optimist. And failed. "I saw you this afternoon, playing with the children. A very charming scene."

Bentley took another long swallow from his glass. He had the look of a man determined to get drunk. "The children are the best part of my occupation. If I save one or two from this place, then my existence will be justified."

Layla tried not to notice the wine stain dribbling down his front. "What do you mean by *save them?*"

"Convince them to think beyond the haven. To spread their wings and fly once they have grown."

"I would think that was an easy task. Aren't the young naturally adventurous?"

"Not unless the seed of curiosity is planted. In a place surrounded by peril, that can be a hard task." He finished his wine. "My apologies. I have a sudden desire to go see an old friend who should have flown away and not looked back. Good night, Miss McHugh."

And the mage left. That sort of abruptness was new. She was prepared to be offended until Hardwin arrived to glare at the mage's retreating back.

"Good riddance," he said. "I'd get rid of that drunkard, but we need him to maintain the wards."

The venom in Hardwin's tone surprised her. "Mage Bentley seems pleasant enough."

"He's here because not even the Conclave could tame his insubordination. Remember that. Bentley is not as harmless as he appears, and not someone a newcomer should spend time with."

"Noted," Layla replied over the rim of her glass.

"Speaking of risky behavior, I heard you went to the jail this afternoon."

She finally took a slow sip of her wine, which was of reasonable quality. "Do your watchmen report all your visitors' movements?"

"When those visitors arrive with a wanted criminal." Hardwin's smile was full of regret.

"Believe me when I say that I had no idea of Mr. Palmer's history here. I was shocked." That much at least was true. "Now I am here and without protection."

"Not true." Hardwin's expression softened. "I fully believe you have a card or two to play yet. Do it right, and you'll enjoy everything this town has to offer."

Layla tipped her chin down to regard Hardwin through her lashes. "But isn't this place full of dangers?"

He leaned so close that the warmth of his body crawled over her skin. "There are creatures in the woods and River Rats sail the waterways. What you need to remember, Miss McHugh, is the real danger is people who don't know their place."

"Have we returned to Mr. Palmer?" She gave a teasing smile. "Or are you are determined to scold me?"

He placed a hand at the small of her back, running his fingertips over the ribs of her corset. "Our acquaintance has begun. I'd like it to continue on a good note."

She leaned into the pressure of his hand, welcoming his attention in a way that was at once immediate but invisible to anyone else in the room. His eyes grew dark as he drew another inch closer.

"Tell me," she began, "I may be done with Mr. Palmer, but I am curious about what happened all those years ago. Were you here when he left Wilcolme Haven?"

"No, I arrived quite a bit later, but I heard the stories. From all accounts, Sam Babbington terrorized those Palmer boys, especially the younger one." Hardwin shuffled restlessly, as if recalling his own childhood nightmares. "The lad grew up, but never fully recovered. I understand why Liam Palmer stuck a knife in Babbington's heart."

"Are you certain he is guilty?"

Hardwin frowned. "He ran, didn't he? And there has to be a

reckoning. Without the law, the havens balance on a cliff's edge of civilization. This is a hard, desperate place."

Layla's stomach tightened. She'd planned to bargain for Palmer's freedom, but bending Hardwin to her will would be more difficult than she'd hoped. For a long, uncomfortable moment, she wasn't sure what to say.

She was saved from having to invent something when the young maid who'd answered the door approached.

Hardwin dropped his hand from Layla's back. "What is it, Mary?"

The girl made an awkward curtsy. "You're wanted in the front parlor, sir. An unexpected guest has arrived."

Hardwin stiffened, his nostrils flaring in annoyance. "Very well."

The maid scurried from the room.

Hardwin lifted Layla's fingers to his lips, leaving a slow kiss. "Excuse me while I attend to this regrettable interruption."

Layla studied the mayor as he threaded his way through the crowded room. There was something familiar about him, the set of his head and the way he moved. An intensity that spoke of nerves carefully disciplined—and now rattled by the maid's message. Whoever the new arrival was, they were not welcome, and that made them interesting.

Setting her glass aside, she began a circuit of the company, following the mayor without seeming to do so. Hardwin wouldn't go far, so she could afford to take her time. This was her opportunity to exchange polite nothings and play the wide-eyed newcomer. She paused once at the refreshments to sample a tiny cracker layered with shaved ham and apple. It was plain fare, but she was hungry.

A minute later, she slipped from the room and retraced her steps toward the main door, hopeful she could trace Hardwin's path. It didn't take long. Male voices drew her to a doorway on the left. She approached on tiptoe, hugging the wall so that she could see without being seen. Thankfully, the lack of servants meant no one else was roaming the halls.

The door was ajar, but only a few inches. Layla's view was confined to the corner of a billiards table and a dreary painting of a ruined building somewhere in the Outlands. She inched closer and was rewarded as Hardwin crossed her field of vision, a billiards cue in his white-knuckled hand.

"Why are you back here? Wouldn't the cities have more use for your particular talents? Or didn't we pay you sufficiently?"

Layla caught a flash of a checked wool in shades of mustard. Whoever this was had no taste in fashion.

"This is my home," the man replied in a light tenor voice. "I have business here, and given your obligations to our city friends, you're in no position to argue."

"Get on whatever vessel you can find leaving here, and do it quickly. Bloody hell, pay the River Rats to take you."

"You don't let them dock in town anymore, or did you forget that?"

"I don't need more magic users underfoot," Hardwin growled. "Too many surprises."

"And yet inconvenient for travel."

"They stop a half-mile downriver, regular as a timepiece. Find them there. Or take an airship. I don't care."

"And if I don't leave?" the visitor asked, a sneer in his tone. He had to be young, to sound that snide. "I had orders to come here, you know. The higher-ups were pleased with our performance. They want more."

Hardwin's response was frigid. "Then get what you need and leave. The havens are a bad place to be unwanted."

"You would know."

Breath catching in her throat, Layla shifted position, hoping for a glimpse of the visitor's face. His words smacked of blackmail, or at least shared guilt. Her fingers itched to nudge the door open another inch, but she'd been caught by creaking hinges in the past. Instead, she risked a more direct glance through the opening, but only caught the back of the dreadful mustard suit. She breathed a curse and drew away.

Someone was coming down the hall—a woman, by the light, fast steps. The sound was coming from the direction of the party. Layla hurried the other way, moving fast to stay out of sight. She paused long enough to try a door, but it was locked. Not surprising, given Hardwin's passion for security. She didn't bother testing any others.

The steps grew louder. The house wasn't that large, but the corridor seemed to go on forever without intersecting another passage. When she finally found one, she whisked around the corner and waited just long enough to see Mrs. Cartwright storm past, clearly in a temper. Had she seen her lover and Layla both leave the room and assumed the worst? Was she hunting for them, hoping and fearing to catch them in a delicate moment?

The notion was almost funny, but not quite. Layla imagined the woman's life, trapped in this futureless place with monsters circling the town. Hardwin, with money and influence, must have looked like an airlift out—and here came a young, pretty stranger, poised to snatch that hope away.

Damn Hardwin, and damn the haven. She was getting out of this town.

She would circle back to the library by a different route, so as not to encounter Hardwin or his jilted mistress. She followed the corridor where she'd hidden past what looked like a series of storage closets. It was dark enough she had to feel her way in places, but her sense of direction, for once, held true. She emerged into the front hall where she'd arrived with Mrs. Bethany.

More footsteps. Layla was halfway across the entrance, and now it sounded as if Mrs. Cartwright was coming up from behind her. She began to hurry forward, but there were men's voices ahead. Hardwin and his visitor were on the move. She cast a defeated look at the front door, with its series of heavy locks, and groaned.

The furniture in the hall was sparse—a hat stand, a mirror, and a bench. None were suitable for hiding behind. The voices were staying where they were, but close enough that she couldn't risk going toward the library. They were probably saying something important, but she was too anxious to listen. Mrs. Cartwright's quick footsteps were headed this way. The woman most likely heard Hardwin's voice, too, and was coming to see what he was up to.

Desperate, Layla grasped the heavy knob of the front door and pulled, not expecting it to budge. Miraculously, it swung open on silent hinges as the cold night air rushed in.

"Hardwin?" Mrs. Cartwright's call was high-pitched and hard with anxiety—and far too close.

Layla slipped outside. *Safe*. The door shut behind her with a faint click. Layla pressed her ear against the thick wood. She couldn't hear Mrs. Cartwright's voice, but that might mean nothing. Experimentally, she turned the handle to open the door just a crack. It didn't budge. In his quest for security, Hardwin had installed a door that locked automatically, even when the deadbolts weren't engaged.

And now she was trapped outside. The temperature had dropped, leaving her shivering. She hated Wilcolme Haven and everyone in it.

Layla pressed her forehead against the chilly wood, debating the merits of pounding on the door versus walking back to the inn. She'd just about decided on the latter when a faint noise in the dark made her turn.

There, under the bright, touchable stars, crouched an Unseen.

CHAPTER 7

Revulsion twisted Layla's gut as she backed against the door. The hairless thing crouched in the dirt, so hunched and twisted that it moved on all fours like a beast. It lifted its head, sniffing the air, as a string of saliva dripped from its chin. With a sudden stab of fear, Layla grabbed the door handle again, rattling the latch without fully turning her back to the creature.

The noise agitated the Unseen enough that it bared its needle-like teeth. Layla gave up on the handle—and any hopes of avoiding Hardwin and his guests—and simply pounded on the door until the creature took a lurching step forward. The sound it made was somewhere between a growl and a whine, reminding her of a famished dog. Then it skittered back, afraid to approach but too hungry to turn away.

Layla's pulse sped. She'd fought Unseen before as part of a team, but she'd had proper weapons and clothes that let her move. At the moment, she was hobbled by a mile of muslin and lace. Sweat trickled down the hollow of her spine.

Frustrated, she gave the door an extra thump with her high-heeled boot. What few servants the mayor had must have gone back to the party. There were no windows to break to get inside. She was on her own.

With a tremor of panic, Layla fumbled open her reticule, the catch suddenly awkward in her hand. At last, her fingers closed on the ivory grip of her pocket pistol—the one she carried in case of unruly clients. She pulled it free, the moonlight gleaming on the tiny barrel. The entire weapon was barely six inches long and held only two shots.

Anger flashed over the Unseen's sunken features. It flung open its arms with a bark of defiance, the rags of its sleeves flapping like wings—and rushed for the stairs and her.

Layla fired, the tiny pistol making a feeble cough. The Unseen reeled back, blood darkening the rags fluttering from its left arm. Her second bullet missed altogether. She hurled the pistol at its head, finally landing a blow. That distracted it just long enough for her to slide her hand through a slit in the seam of her skirts. Cold panic clawed her gut as she groped for the knife she wore strapped to her thigh. Her fingers found the hilt, but it tangled in the forest of her petticoats when she tried to drag it free.

The Unseen thundered up the steps toward her. She was trapped, the locked door at her back. She skittered sideways, boot soles sliding on the wooden boards in her effort to twist away. The Unseen jabbed its talons through the cage of her bustle and used it as a lever to jerk her off her feet. Layla went down in a rustling heap, but the motion freed her knife. She slashed upward, and the Unseen recoiled in surprise.

Its head exploded as a thunderclap tore the night in two. *Gunfire.* Layla scrambled away, shrinking into the corner of the porch as blood and bone spattered the boards. A fetid stink fogged the air as the Unseen's body tumbled down the steps. Layla pushed herself upright, every limb shaking.

Now that the Unseen sprawled unmoving below, she could see it wore the rags of an aeronaut's uniform, maybe from one of the airships that vanished every year. No wonder Palmer hated flying over the Outlands.

She looked beyond the crumpled body. Mayor Hardwin strolled into view, a large, heavy pistol dangling loosely in his hand. Layla leaned against the side of the house as she slowly pushed herself upright on wobbly legs. She slipped the knife back in its sheath before she dropped it.

Hardwin came to a halt at the bottom of the steps. "I heard your knocking, Miss McHugh. It's not safe to wander alone after dark, even with a mage on site to keep the wards fresh."

"All I wanted was a breath of fresh air." In truth, Layla struggled to fill her lungs. Panic still squeezed her like a fist. "I'm not used to the lack of windows."

"One grows accustomed." He climbed the steps and took her arm, gripping her above the elbow. "The same way one gets into the habit of keeping the doors locked against visitors from the forest. Some are quite capable of stealing in and making a meal of a family in their beds."

Layla's mind balked at that image. "But you have a mage. And wards."

"Bentley's magic occasionally falters. He has unfortunate habits." With a firm hand, he guided her down the stairs. "As do you, Miss McHugh."

"What—"

"You're a clever spy, but I learned long ago how to detect eavesdroppers."

Layla fell silent as he steered her to a modest door at the side of the house—no doubt the one he'd used when he came to her rescue. Again, familiarity nagged at her. She'd seen Mayor Hardwin somewhere before.

He ushered her through to a well-appointed office that was far nicer than Palmer's interview room on Gryphon Avenue, and yet somehow the same. A heavy desk occupied pride of place.

Hardwin sat behind it and gestured to the armchair meant for visitors.

"Are you injured?" he asked, setting his pistol on the desktop and pushing it to one side. It clunked against the base of a heavy brass lamp. Beside the lamp was an inkpot and a box of bullets.

"No," Layla replied. "You arrived in time."

"Good." He sat back, toying with a cufflink.

"Should you tell someone about the Unseen? Explain the gunshot?"

"No one questions the sound of a gun firing in these parts. Not this close to the forest."

"And the body?"

"It can wait for daylight." He flicked his fingers at an imaginary corpse. "For now, tell me what you're so desperate to learn that you nearly fed yourself to the monsters."

Lila studied the oak paneling over Hardwin's head. There was a bullet hole right where the trim met the coffered ceiling. "I confess I was exploring the house without permission. When I heard someone coming, I went outside to escape notice."

"And locked yourself outside." He nodded. "What did Palmer think you'd find?"

"Palmer?"

"Come now, you arrived with him, and I know you paid a visit to his cell. Given his history here, I don't believe he came here out of a sense of nostalgia. There was a reason."

What was the best way to play this game? Layla shifted in the armchair, nervous energy running wild. Perhaps she needed to treat him like a client, whetting his eagerness for the final reward. There was an art to surrender while stealing away the reins of the situation.

"I came here of my own accord," she said. "I am searching for a man who visited Londria. Rumor has it that this was his home town."

"Who?" It was a question, but Hardwin's tone said he already knew the answer.

"The name he used was Polliver."

He leaned forward, palms flat on the desk. "Forget you ever heard of him."

"He was here at your house tonight. That's why you left the library."

He shot her a warning look.

Layla played her hunch. "I had to ask myself why Detective Inspector Palmer was sidelined the moment he stepped off the airship."

"Are you going to beg for the detective's life?" Hardwin asked dryly. "I wouldn't think he could afford someone like you."

Layla stiffened, but she let the comment go. Palmer didn't need her to beg; he needed her to use her wits. "Someone wants him off the case. That pleads his innocence far better than I ever could."

"I wouldn't know about his guilt or innocence. Palmer left Wilcolme Haven before I got here. That said, it suits me to have him out from underfoot."

"And there is the second mystery," Layla said, closing in on her quarry. "How does a newcomer come to power in a closed community like this? One who sets up an armed watch and yet keeps few servants? One who is at once used to hard physical labor and yet casually displays priceless art?"

His expression didn't change. "I've made my way like any self-made man. I supply whatever people need or want, if the price is right. Sometimes I locate materials, and other times I find people with special skills."

Including saboteurs? "And how do you manage that in a backwater like Wilcolme Haven?"

"With great imagination." He waved a careless hand.

"I would say with great care. I heard you moved the airfield close to town so that you can observe who comes and goes."

"I did the same with water traffic. If the River Rats want to trade, they do it a half-mile downriver."

"I take it you don't like competition."

"I like interference even less. This is *my* town." He smiled now, more with his eyes than his lips. Whatever game he was playing, he thought he'd won.

"It's certainly a step up for you." She shrugged. "Londria is smaller than one assumes. I remember seeing you at Lord Warren's card parties."

"You mean his private gambling hell," Hardwin countered, his triumph visibly fading.

"He is the Prime Minister," she replied. "It is the best quality of hell."

"One I gratefully escaped." He studied Layla's face, tracing each feature with his gaze. No doubt he was trying to recall her face, but who really looked at the women there simply to provide pleasure?

"You lost everything and ran. Then you started your empire all over again in the havens, where you'd clearly prefer to be left alone. How did you get entangled with the *Leopard* affair?"

Hardwin shrugged. "My old friends found me. They demanded a favor for keeping my location to themselves."

Layla caught her breath. She knew the type. Londria was rife with criminal brotherhoods—organized, ruthless, and coated in a veneer of hard cash.

"They needed you to supply someone with certain talents. You sent them Polliver."

"They weren't the ones who made the plans, just those who were ordered to see it done."

"And you owed them a debt."

"Precisely." He picked up the pistol. "They tracked me into the Outlands to demand their pound of flesh. Imagine what they will do if someone exposes them now."

"All the more reason to control who comes to visit."

"Correct." Lamplight kissed the gleaming barrel as he pointed it straight between her eyes. "Information has a price, Miss McHugh."

⌒

Palmer woke at the rattle of his cell door. When it opened, a blazing lantern obscured the tall figure who carried it.

"Damn it all, Liam," said a voice he'd all but forgotten. "I heard you were here."

Palmer sat up fast enough to make his head swim. He gripped the edge of the bench and forced the surprise from his voice. "Councilor Bentley."

The mage set the lantern on the cell floor, illuminating the dark-blue fabric of his rumpled robes. "Not many use that title any longer. You make me feel old."

The man had aged, at least when compared with Palmer's memories. There was white in his unkempt hair and a web of lines on his face. But his hawkish features were the same, as was the acrid smell of liquor clinging to his breath.

"Is it time for my confession?" Palmer asked lightly.

"Not my remit," the mage said, folding his long arms. "My job is to preserve the wards, not your soul. You know that."

"Then what brings you here?" Palmer sucked in a deep breath, finally letting a mix of joy and sadness reach his heart.

The mage had been one of the few adults who had treated him with kindness. He'd brought the children treats—sugar rock and licorice—and told them stories whenever they escaped their chores on a long summer evening. Palmer had assumed Bentley died from drink long ago.

"Perhaps I wanted to see what you'd made of yourself, Detective Inspector Palmer. Now there's a laugh."

"I'm good at what I do," Palmer shot back, then regretted it. He wasn't ten years old. He didn't need to explain his choices.

"You could have written."

"But I did not and, yes, I feel guilty."

"I suppose you had your reasons," Bentley said with a shrug. "I can imagine you valued the separation between who you were and who you became. There is a strange power in our former lives, as if one touch of their essence could crumble our present selves to dust."

Palmer changed the subject. "How is Kieran?"

"He's still at the workshop. You did the right thing, setting him up. He flourished. Maybe one day he'll take on a student of his own."

Relief hit Palmer like a fist to the chest. He sagged against the filthy wall. "You helped."

Bentley shook his head. "Only with the formalities. You did the work. You made sure he was protected at your own expense."

Palmer looked away, refusing to acknowledge a momentary flash of resentment. That's not who he was. Kieran deserved whatever help he got. "Don't tell my brother I'm here. I don't want him mixed up in this."

"Your choice." With cracking knees, the mage sat down on the bench, almost where Layla had sat before.

Palmer missed the woman with a pang he couldn't afford to examine.

The mage pulled out a flask and unscrewed the top. "Drink?"

Palmer shook his head. He recognized the sharp aroma of Bentley's own distillation—a clear brew that gave waking nightmares to the unwary.

The mage tipped the flask to his lips and took a long swallow. Then he wiped his mouth on his sleeve. "I hear they've accused you of murder," Bentley said quietly.

"Do you believe them?"

Bentley shrugged. "Not your priest, remember?"

Palmer's hands flexed, itching to shake the man. "What are they saying?"

"The blade that did the stabbing came from Marvelle's workshop. I don't know what it was used for. I mean, its use beyond stopping a human heart." Bentley took another mouthful of drink.

"Marvelle was too old for murder. He could barely walk."

"You made an excellent suspect, given your history with Babbington and your sudden departure that same night. The River Rats were also popular scapegoats. There was a boat at the town dock that night—there always had been, at least until the mayor said otherwise—but those folk are hard to catch. Much easier to accuse a local boy."

"Babbington had no dealings with the River Rats. He despised them."

The mage shrugged again. "And so we're back to you."

"Conviction by default. That's Wilcolme's justice all over. Never changes." Palmer grabbed the flask from Bentley's hand and drank. The liquid burned his throat. He spluttered a moment, eyes watering. "Blast it, that brew is worse than back alley grog."

Bentley plucked the flask from Palmer's hand. "Give it a moment."

The heat of it hit Palmer's stomach, radiating out like a miniature sun. He floated on the sensation for a delicious moment before settling back into his body. "Bloody hell."

Bentley chuckled and put the flask away. "Half spell, half distillery. This last batch can double as fuel for a fireworks display. Such whimsical experiments cure the boredom of exile."

"Londria's Conclave can't condemn you to serve the havens any longer. You could leave."

"The Conclave is bigger than Londria, and the High Council of all the mages do not forgive rebellion. The only rung below service in the havens is death."

"Then why let you live?"

"I was too valuable to waste. My presence here allows a

productive haven to thrive." The mage waved the notion aside with one long-fingered hand. "It's better this way. I can keep watch on the feral vermin who make this dunghill their kingdom. Occasionally I can prevent them from eating their young."

Palmer nodded, remembering how Bentley had done his best to shield him from the horrific details of his parents' death. "Those young vermin are grateful, as I was."

Bentley was silent for a long time, and when he finally spoke, he changed the subject. "I met your woman tonight."

Palmer closed his eyes. "She's not my woman."

"You should change that."

"I'll be forest meat soon."

"You're a detective tonight, Liam m'boy." Bentley rose. "Prove you committed no crime."

"Babbington died a decade ago. I don't remember much."

"Yes, you do. I think every outrage you suffered in Wilcolme Haven is burned into you like a brand." Bentley knocked lightly on the cell door, then turned back to Palmer. "It's up to you to change that. Then you can leave here for good. Hopefully alive."

"And you say you're not a confessor," Palmer snapped as the door opened and Bentley stepped outside.

"I can't abide whining," Bentley shot back as the cell door closed. "Give me a tale for the ages. One I can drink to."

"Why not just save me? You're a mage. You have the power."

"So do you. And I'm not in the business of conjuring innocence."

"Then why did you come?"

"I told you that already. I wanted to see who you were now. The rest is up to you. I won't be back."

And then the mage was gone. At least he'd left the lantern. Palmer slumped back on the bench, surprisingly clear-headed. Bentley's wicked brew had shocked his system so thoroughly he could think for the first time since his arrest.

He hadn't exactly been whining, but he took the mage's point.

Arriving back in the haven had disoriented him. He'd been floundering like a landed fish, hooked and gasping.

But Bentley's visit had reminded him of that rebel lad who'd boarded an airship to parts unknown. He'd fought for his survival before and won.

Leave here for good. Hopefully alive. It wasn't much, but it was the start of a plan.

CHAPTER 8

*P*almer craned his neck, staring at the top of the cell wall. He'd forgotten what it was like to live in a place without windows, to never be able to look beyond the horizon of one's own wall. That explained a lot about the havens he'd never considered until that moment—but philosophy wasn't his main concern.

He needed information. When he'd been delivered to the prison, they'd thrust a bag over his head. It would be very useful to know where he was before he tried to plan an escape. Happily, prisons stank and required something for ventilation, so the town worthies put windows in the cells. They were tiny, high, and horizontal—and useless for escape—but they were still windows with monster-proof iron grills bolted to their frames. No glass, of course. That would be too expensive to transport this far from the city.

The opening he was looking at was a long way from the floor in a room with no furniture to repurpose as a ladder. His only option was to climb the bare bricks. He could already feel the aches and bruises.

Again, he wished for his cigarettes and lighter. He'd taken up smoking mostly because Babbington had forbidden anyone to touch the ornate stoppered jar of tobacco that stood on the mantel of his study. Stealing it was the kind of petty revenge available to a lad in his early teens. Bad habit. Stupid reasons.

Palmer pulled off his boots and socks, wondering idly if he was setting himself up to break his own neck. Maybe this was a foolish idea born from the fumes of Bentley's brew—he was fairly sure it contained some of the hallucinogens the River Rats used. They traded with the mage for pots of magefire and other magical wares—mostly illegal, of course. Whatever the case, at least Palmer was no longer bored.

He approached the wall, feeling for gaps between the bricks. He could do nothing while under lock and key. Escape, investigate, find Polliver, protect Layla—every course of action required freedom of movement. This was enemy territory, and playing by the rules would do him no good.

Working his fingers and toes between the bricks, he began to climb. His brain told him it was only a dozen feet or so, but the light was so bad it felt like clawing his way through immeasurable darkness. Closing his eyes, he used what his fingertips told him instead. The bricks were hard, sharp-edged and new, confirming that the jail had been built since he'd left the haven. But the workers hadn't done a proper job, because the mortar was uneven. He could feel the cool night air seeping through the cracks and used it to find his next finger and toehold.

The presence of the new jail was interesting, as well as the uniformed watchmen. Yes, there had always been town security, but nothing like this. Someone—presumably the new mayor—was nervous. Given that Polliver had come from this place, Wilcolme Haven had somehow gone from rural cesspit to rural cesspit with connections to bigger concerns. Londria-sized concerns, with exploding airships.

Which made an interesting intersection with his own problems. Why dredge up a decade-old murder? Was it to sideline an inconvenient detective? One who was about to pull on the thread that connected the town to the dangerous visitors with bigger concerns? As likely as that seemed, there had to be something more—some report, some scrap of evidence from the old crime—to make an accusation plausible.

If the watchman who arrested Palmer could be believed, someone had pointed at Palmer ten years ago and accused him of murder. Who would have done it?

He had to work this like any other case, and that meant starting with what he knew. At the time, someone clearly found Babbington's body with physical evidence that a murder had taken place. According to Bentley, they'd also found the murder weapon, a knife.

Who was around back then to serve as suspects? Marvelle, the clockmaker, was too infirm to attack a healthy man like the schoolteacher. Kieran had been small for his age, so he wasn't a likely candidate. The former mayor had been Babbington's friend. The butcher, Cartwright? He actually had the size and skill, but no. Babbington's real enemies were the children he taught, and he never bullied those with strong protectors. He had been too smart for that. Bentley was correct—no one was as easy to blame as Palmer, a young orphan who'd suffered under Babbington's so-called care.

Palmer's fingers gripped the bottom ledge of the window. The ledge was almost two feet wide—not a proper window frame but a simple absence of bricks. Levering himself up with his left hand, he grabbed for the iron grill with his right, hoping the bolts were secure enough to bear his weight. His fingers closed on the cold metal, and with a heave, he shifted his left hand from the gritty sill to fasten on the iron bars as well. From there, he pulled himself up until he could brace his elbows on the deep sill and peer out.

It was his first proper look at Wilcolme Haven since he'd arrived. It was too dark to see much, but there was a pool of light from the lantern above the jail's front door. It illuminated a swath of ground that included the path leading into the town. There were other lights, too, dotted like fireflies through the town. With no windows streaming lights after dark, the town had always been good about putting lanterns on the street corners.

The spring-bright scent of the river rode on the breeze, reminding him of a thousand childhood nights fetching water for the evening chores. In the distance, voices rose and then disappeared as a pair of watchmen passed by. The familiar accent of the havens tugged at something inside Palmer—not nostalgia, not a sense of home, never that—but a profound recognition of place.

His calves and shoulders ached from bracing himself on the ledge. He was about to let go when a figure emerged from the darkness, moving at a brisk pace. Palmer's line of sight didn't extend to the man's destination, but the coat and valise suggested he was hurrying away from the airfield. Palmer squinted, cursing the shadows, until the figure passed close to the lantern outside the jail. The yellow light washed over the man's features, revealing one of the faces from the gallery case. Palmer's fingers tightened on the grill.

Polliver. Where was the man going in such a hurry? Had he just learned that no aeronaut worth his goggles would lift off at night this deep into the forest? This wasn't Londria, with well-lit airfields and miles of city to land in if the ascent failed. Plus, some flying creatures loved a nighttime snack, and anything below the tree canopy was fair game.

Whatever his reasons, Polliver was marching toward the town with purpose. Palmer clenched his jaw in frustration. He'd finally found his quarry and couldn't do a thing about it. He hitched himself an inch higher on the wide ledge, straining for a better look at Polliver before he disappeared into the night.

The brick beneath his right elbow wrenched free of the mortar, crashing onto the floor. Palmer let go of the bars with one hand, grabbing for the wall. The sudden shift in balance was too much. Another brick came away in his hand, and he fell to the prison floor.

Palmer rolled as he hit the ground, eventually crashing into the foot of the bench and barely missing the lantern. He remained there a moment, sucking air back into his lungs. With the brick still clutched in his hand, he got to his feet, relieved that all his limbs still worked. Experimentally, he felt the back of his head. No blood, but he'd have a headache for a while.

Footfalls sounded outside the door. The watchman on duty must have heard the fall. Palmer backed away, hugging the wall and taking a firmer hold of the brick. When the key rattled in the heavy lock, he barely heard it over his thundering pulse.

~

LAYLA HELD HARDWIN'S GAZE, desperate to find some scrap of humanity she could exploit. She might as well have locked eyes with a statue. Or an empty vault. The affable public figure he presented to the haven's citizens was long gone. The gun pointed straight at her didn't waver.

"Did I really ask too many questions, Mr. Hardwin?" Though her pounding pulse made it hard to breathe, Layla kept her tone light. "You volunteered your information rather quickly. Am I being punished simply because you wanted to talk?"

The corners of his mouth turned down. "There is no profit in withholding information when someone is creeping through the hallways to learn my secrets. If you are reasonably good at your craft, Miss McHugh, you will find out what you want to know."

"So, you have saved us both some time."

He gave a brief nod. "Rather than worry about questions, I eliminate the questioner. It's more efficient that way."

Layla's breath caught. This was a death sentence, and with

Palmer in prison, there was no hope of rescue. If word of their fate ever reached Londria, it would be far too late to matter.

"Why not let the Unseen have me?" she asked, desperate to keep him talking.

"This is my town, and it was hunting on my patch." A smile flickered across his face, then was gone. "I am pragmatic, but there are some standards that must be observed."

"Then satisfy my curiosity on one more point," she said, smoothing her skirts. The heel of her hand brushed the knife, the steel hilt reassuringly solid.

"What, no cries of protest? No pleas for your life?" He sounded vaguely bored, but lowered the gun.

She slid her hand through her skirts to grasp her weapon. She prayed the angle of the desk hid the motion from Hardwin's view. "I don't beg," she replied. "Do me the courtesy of remembering we are, in our way, both professionals."

"My apologies," he said dryly.

"Who hired your friends?" She slid the knife free and positioned it so that the blade was concealed. "Who wanted to destroy the *Leopard*?"

"I don't know," Hardwin replied, rising from his seat. "At the time, I did not care. Now I confess to a degree of curiosity. I wish I had asked."

"Pity." She remained where she was, frozen with indecision. She'd fought the Unseen, but the mayor was a more complicated monster.

He gestured toward the door with his pistol. "It is time to go, Miss McHugh. Although I do not tolerate ravening abominations within the haven, I am perfectly happy to send a gift to their own territory."

"I'd prefer a clean death."

"I'd prefer not to clean." He waved the gun again. "If you would oblige."

She surged from her seat, using momentum to drive the knife

point toward his heart. Hardwin flinched backward, spoiling her aim even as she used her left hand to swat his pistol aside. The knife point struck his pocket watch and slid downward, skewering his guts. He doubled over, making a strangled wheeze. Layla snatched the heavy glass inkpot from the desk and smashed it down just behind his ear.

Hardwin dropped to the carpet. Layla stared at his still form, her thoughts stalling like an engine out of steam. Then, with a sudden lurch of energy, she snatched up his pistol, thrusting it through the sash of her dress. Then she grabbed the box of bullets for good measure. She'd chosen a course of action. All that remained was to carry it through.

Dropping to her knees, she searched him for keys that might belong to Palmer's cell. She found coins, keys, a money clip, and a watch. She thrust everything into her skirt pockets, distributing the weight as best she could, and wrenched her knife free. It came loose with a squelch and rivulet of blood. A wave of revulsion coursed through her, and she lunged for the door and fresh air.

She had to free Palmer and find a way out of the haven. However casual the townsfolk were about Unseen corpses and gunshots, it wouldn't be long before someone started looking for the mayor.

After she closed the side door behind her, she glanced toward the night sky. The moon was setting, which put the time well past midnight. No doubt the party would break up soon.

She gripped her knife and sped into the darkness.

CHAPTER 9

Palmer swung the brick, striking the watchman on the side of his skull. The man went down with a grunt, but instantly groped for a handhold to pull himself up again. With a sharp stab of guilt, Palmer caught him with a hard cross to the jaw. This time, the watchman stayed down, limbs splayed like a sleeping child. He'd have a fierce headache in the morning.

Palmer stripped off the man's belt and bound his hands, then gathered up the keys and Bentley's lantern, locking the cell door behind him as he prowled toward the front office. The morning shift would find the watchman in the cell, but with luck, Palmer would have long vanished.

The building was silent, with only a single oil lamp illuminating the watchman's desk. The light penciled in the edges of the furniture and spilled over a scatter of paperwork and the crumbs from a half-eaten meat pie. A mouse darted away at his approach, mouth stuffed with pastry. Palmer set the lantern down and rummaged in a row of cubbyholes behind the desk. There, he found his watch, lighter, and identification. His cash was gone. He cursed inwardly, but there was no time to search for it.

The watchman's keys unlocked a battered metal weapons cabinet. Palmer pulled open the door with a whine of old hinges and regarded a row of crossbows. Faint light gilded the brass gears and levers that allowed an archer to quickly reload and fire. Every child of the haven learned to shoot, and he'd had a knack for it. With the reflex of long practice, he chose a bow and tested the draw. He would have preferred a rifle, but this would do. The bow had a long leather strap, frayed and supple with use. He slung the weapon over his shoulder, grabbed a quiver of bolts, and sped from the building, keeping to the shadows.

For an instant, he considered trying his luck at the dock. He could steal a boat or—far better—beg a ride from the River Rats. But he would not leave Layla behind, and there was his brother to consider. The brother who, with his help, had taken an apprenticeship with a master clockmaker. And that last point raised more questions.

Palmer had to face the truth, not just as a sibling, but as a detective, too. With Marvelle dead, who here except Kieran had the expertise to build the device that had destroyed the *Leopard*? Kieran had never known how to protect himself, and a certain kind of gutter-dweller could scent that weakness from a mile away. He could have been coerced, or even corrupted.

And Palmer hadn't been around to protect him. Guilt rose in a hot, prickling wave. He had to make things right. First, he would apologize to Kieran for leaving him behind, even if it had seemed the right thing to do at the time. And then he would ask whether his brother had ever met Polliver.

He stopped at the corner of the jail, waiting for his pounding pulse to slow. The night smelled of river mud and the tang of coming rain. Time vanished and he was twelve again, hands raw from scrubbing the schoolroom floors. He'd been hungry then, too.

Palmer studied the pale ribbon of the dirt path, calculating the distance to where he thought Marvelle's old workshop should be. A faint footfall sounded nearby, making him startle like a cat.

"Palmer." It came as a stage whisper.

"Miss McHugh?" he replied. "What are you doing here?"

There was an exasperated pause. "What do you think? I came to rescue you."

Surprise parted his lips, but sarcasm came to his rescue. "Thoughtful of you."

"How did you escape?" she demanded.

"Shall we save the explanation for later?" He began to walk.

She followed. "Is it a good one?"

"I'll tell you when there are fewer unconscious victims in my wake."

"Fair enough." Layla stepped into the moonlight, her hair loose and with a huge pistol thrust through the sash of her tattered dress. By the set of her jaw, she was in a terrifying mood.

Palmer's insides gave a strange lurch that contained a pinch of awe.

"I would like to leave now, please," Layla said in a low voice. "Country life doesn't suit me."

"That may be difficult. My choices are limited by the fact that I've been accused of murder."

"I suppose that makes public transportation somewhat awkward."

They came to a halt under a stand of elms that screened the jail from the nearest buildings. All he could see of Layla's face was the curve of her cheek and brow. The rest was shadow.

"Who knows you came to get me?" Palmer asked.

"No one."

"Then you may leave on the next airship."

"I don't think so."

The errant light caught the silver spill of her tears. Mesmerized, Palmer reached out and cupped her face in both hands, sweeping the wetness away with his thumbs. A heartbeat later, he realized they were standing inches apart—and he wished those inches to perdition. The urge to bend down and steal a kiss was all but overwhelming, but men stole from women like Layla far too often. She deserved better.

"What happened?" he asked gently.

She pulled away, turning her face to the darkness. "Let's just say I'm as much a fugitive as you are."

He caught her shoulders, steadying her as he might a skittish animal. By the state of her clothes, she'd been in a fight. "Are you hurt?"

Her laugh was bitter. "The last man who asked me that—"

"I'm not him," Palmer cut in. "And I'm asking because we're about to run for our lives, and I need to know if you're wounded."

"I can run."

"Good."

She turned back to him, fisting her hands in the fabric of his jacket. "But I am afraid."

He put his hands over hers, giving them a gentle squeeze. "That's only sensible."

She caught her breath. "What do we do?"

Palmer forced himself to sound calm. "We stop for supplies, then we run."

"Where do we get supplies?"

Palmer cursed inwardly, guilt rising one more time. He didn't want Kieran involved, but at the same time he had to find out what his brother knew. "My brother's workshop. He'll have what we need."

"And then we go?"

Palmer gave a curt nod. "We head for the river. If we can't go by air, it's our only chance. The Unseen don't venture into the water."

She stepped back. "We need to hurry."

Something had happened—something that put fear in the line

of her mouth—but questions could come later. Instead, he led Layla along the dirt paths behind the buildings, avoiding every chance to be seen. Within minutes, they circled a large, squat structure and mounted the steps to Marvelle's Clockwork Emporium. Marvelle himself might be gone, but the old black-and-gold sign with his name was there, along with a wrought-iron bracket bearing a wooden plaque painted with the hexagon and shears. Not everyone in the havens could read, but they all knew the maker's mark.

Palmer turned the heavy brass door handle. It swung outward with a faint creak. The room beyond was lit by a single candle stub sitting on a long workbench that ran down the center of the space. Familiarity struck him like a physical blow. It didn't seem right that the old man was gone. He'd ruled this domain as long as Palmer could remember.

Layla drew the pistol from her sash. "Why is the door unlocked? Isn't everyone afraid of the Unseen?"

"They are." Palmer drew an arrow from his quiver and stepped slowly over the threshold, walking on tiptoe until he reached the center of the room. The place smelled of wood shavings and linseed oil and, beneath that, a faint tang of spoiled food.

Behind the workbench was a counter with rows of drawers below and shelving that reached to the rafters. From long hours spent here as a child, he knew that was where supplies were kept. The cabinets around the rest of the room held pieces for sale or works in progress. The rooms beyond were a combination of living quarters and additional workspaces. He remembered a small forge and a tank for coating objects with silver. Marvelle had let him experiment with both, though under close supervision.

"Odd," Layla murmured. "The candle says someone is present, but I don't hear anyone."

Palmer cursed under his breath. He should have noticed that himself instead of wallowing in memories. Now that he looked around, he could see tools out of place, a scatter of screws left out on the counter. If his brother still lived here, something was wrong. He was tidy to the point of obsession.

"Kieran?" he called, approaching the entrance to the back rooms.

Layla followed a step behind him, watching the workshop's front door for anyone creeping in behind them.

The entrance to the living quarters was down a short, unlit hallway. A sliver of light showed under the connecting door. When there was no answer, he abandoned any further attempt at stealth and simply knocked. The door flew open so suddenly, Layla gave a faint yip of surprise.

Palmer found himself toe to toe with the haven's mage. "Bentley? Where is my brother?"

The mage glanced from Palmer to Layla. "I see you two are still up to your lapels in mayhem. Have they found the mayor's corpse yet? Good riddance to that one."

Palmer's insides turned to ice as he put the pieces together. *Bloody hell.* "What happened?"

Ignoring the question, Layla shifted from her position behind Palmer and trained her weapon on the mage. "How do you know about that?"

Bentley gave a sweeping gesture toward his own person. "I am magical. It is a requirement of the job."

"Bollocks," Palmer snapped. "What happened?"

Bentley shrugged. "No one is certain if the knife wound or the blow to the head finished him."

"I can explain," Layla began, her voice thick with what sounded like dread.

As a detective, he demanded answers, but this wasn't the time. Not when they were on the run. "Stay on point," Palmer ground out. "Where is Kieran?"

Bentley shook his head. "Gone. By the dirty dishes, I'd say he left in a hurry."

"We talked earlier. Why didn't you tell me?"

"I didn't know. The lad keeps to himself."

"I thought you said you're magical."

"Why would he leave so fast?" Layla broke in, finally lowering her gun.

Bentley shifted as the tension in the room eased a notch. "The mayor had visitors. Friends from before he came here, I think. One of them just returned. He goes by Polliver these days, though he grew up in these parts."

"He's not Hardwin's friend," Layla put in. "These men who came are business associates. They were hired to scupper the *Leopard*. Hardwin introduced them to Polliver, and they sent Polliver back here. I think he came to get another incendiary device."

"The mayor told you that?" Palmer asked. "Did he say who his associates were working for? Did he say who made the device?"

Layla shook her head, her eyes wide as if she were trying not to cry. "He said he didn't know who hired his old partners. I think he was telling the truth about that."

Bentley made a derisive noise. "Polliver has the moral compass of a serpent, but hardly the skills to sabotage an airship. That's where your brother enters the picture. He could devise a means to carry out the job."

"No," Palmer said automatically. "Not willingly."

"He may not have had a choice," Layla said gently. "Even Hardwin was scared of these men."

"Precisely," Bentley concluded. "I think when Polliver came back again, Kieran was smart enough to run. He would know they wouldn't leave him alone, especially if he started to look like a loose end."

"That's one possibility, but we need facts." Palmer finally stepped into the living quarters, leaving the workshop behind.

It was little more than a tiny kitchen leading to a bedroom. Dirty dishes covered a table pushed up against the wall. As

Bentley had observed, the mess looked about a week old. Flies crawled over the stinking pile.

The Kieran he knew would never have tolerated such disorder. He was obsessively neat. If Bentley's theory was correct, he'd been badly distracted for days before he fled. His brother had known something dangerous was on the horizon. Or had he heard what had happened to the *Leopard*, and been swamped with remorse?

The wave of worry Palmer had been pushing away flooded in. The Kieran he knew had no experience in the wider world. Then again, time had passed, and for Kieran it had passed in this cesspool of a place. Palmer didn't actually know what his brother was capable of, and that was his own bloody fault for leaving him behind.

Palmer sank into a chair, suddenly exhausted. "Where would he go?"

Bentley folded his arms. "If I had to guess, Londria. He knew you were there."

"When did Polliver turn up?" Palmer asked.

"I'm not precisely sure, but it was before you arrived. A couple of days, at most."

If Kieran had left shortly after Polliver arrived, the Palmer brothers might both have been in Londria for a few hours. Maybe a day. Surely Palmer would have sensed he was near?

"But how could he leave Wilcolme Haven without the mayor finding out?" Layla asked.

"Kieran made friends among the aeronauts," Bentley replied. "He's repaired enough equipment on those ships over the years. Getting a flight off the books would be child's play."

"Bloody hell." Palmer got to his feet. "If Kieran is gone, then where is Polliver?"

"He was at the mayor's house tonight." Layla's tone was sharp. "I heard Hardwin telling him to get out of town and not come back."

"I saw him walking into town from the airfield." Palmer silently cursed. He'd momentarily forgotten his quarry. "There's still a chance to learn who ordered the sabotage of the *Leopard*."

"Only if you catch him." Bentley pointed toward the open door. "But I doubt you will get the chance."

Layla gasped, whirling toward the door. A heartbeat later, Palmer heard shouts and the snarl of dogs. He ran into the workshop and looked out the window, only to find the moon had set behind a thick layer of clouds. The night was an inky black punctuated by the will-o'-the-wisp flames of distant lanterns.

The racket grew louder as figures emerged from the trees.

He felt Layla's warm presence beside him. "They're coming for us."

CHAPTER 10

"This way." Bentley gestured toward Kieran's living quarters. "Out the back. There's a path to the river."

"Through the forest at night," Palmer countered. "We both know that way is thick with Unseen."

"I'll go with you." Bentley waved a careless hand. "I'm more than capable of warding off a handful of gnashers and, with luck, the River Rats will be on schedule. I'm expecting a boat tonight."

The solution had presented itself a little too neatly for Palmer's liking, but he had no better plan. Layla cast him a doubtful look, but Palmer gently nudged her in Bentley's direction. They hurried back into the kitchen and out the other side through a narrow exit that led into the alley. They followed Bentley's long strides as he led them between two buildings for a dozen yards. Then the buildings abruptly ended in a patch of grass and scrubby bushes.

Bentley cupped his hands together, whispering a word Palmer didn't understand. The breeze turned chill for a moment, swirling around them as light blossomed in his hands. It was not bright like a flame, but diffuse, like the shine of polished silver. As he parted his fingers, it flowed softly over the landscape, revealing a footpath worn through the grass and toward the edge of the woods. There, the trees loomed like angry, hungry sentinels. Palmer's every instinct begged him to back away.

"The river is that way," the mage said, breathing hard. Whether it was from the brisk pace or use of magic, Palmer couldn't tell.

Thunder rumbled from the west. Layla's warm hand slipped into Palmer's. "Do we run and hope for the best?"

"No," Bentley said. "We go as quietly as we can, with a pinch of magic to hide our scent and sound. Follow me."

The mage closed his hands around the light, dimming it until there was no more than a thin veil of light to make out the hazards on the ground. Bentley took the lead, whispering under his breath. Once again, the air swirled around them, cold enough to make Layla shiver at Palmer's side. He peeled off his coat and offered it to her.

"You need the warmth more than I do," he said.

"Are you sure?" But she was already slipping her arms through the sleeves. The coat was too wide through the shoulders, but she hugged it close.

"Apparently, yes." Palmer tugged the hem of his waistcoat into place. The wind bit through his shirtsleeves, but her look of genuine gratitude made the discomfort tolerable.

The cold was the least of their troubles. The sound of the watch grew louder, punctuated by the bark and growl of dogs. These weren't hunting dogs—no one here roamed the countryside in pursuit of game—but huge, heavy-jawed creatures bred for herding and protecting livestock against the Unseen. Palmer kept his expression still, but his pulse sped another degree.

When Bentley stepped beneath the trees, Layla and Palmer hastened to follow. The cold wind trailed their small party as they picked their way over roots and fallen branches, muffling the noise of their passage. Bentley went first, then Layla, with Palmer bringing up the rear.

Palmer had his crossbow at the ready, bolt loaded and ready to fire, while Layla had her pistol drawn. The leaves whispered around them, as if relaying word of strangers in the forest. When he looked up, only a sliver of sky showed between the twisting branches, making the path feel like the passageway to a tomb.

And yet, he saw no glint of eyes among the trees. Bentley's spell was different from the mage magic Palmer had seen in Londria. There, the Conclave of mages had worked in groups, conducting power through silver conduits to keep Unseen from breaching the city wall. Word had it every spell was carefully monitored by the senior mages, with none of the creative experimentation Bentley was known for. Was this the rebellion that had landed him in trouble with the Conclave? Although Palmer had given it little thought as a child, it occurred to him now how powerful Bentley was—and how far he'd fallen to end up here.

They crept along the path for what felt like hours, but was likely no more than twenty minutes. Bentley's spell did not falter, though Palmer's energy began to flag. The cold seeped into his bones and seemed to drain oxygen from the air. Before long, they were all panting as they struggled to keep their footfalls silent. Palmer blinked to keep his vision in focus, his skin creeping as the long fingers of the trees brushed his sleeve. Layla stumbled once, but caught herself with a dancer's grace and a sailor's curse. At long last, Palmer caught the glint of dark water ahead. They were nearing the river.

For the first time, Palmer dared to hope. The nerve-wracking trek through the trees was almost over and a chance of escaping the haven was within reach. Better still, their pursuers were nowhere in sight. As they had pushed deeper into the woods, the barking of the dogs had fallen away. Maybe they had been as wary of the Unseen as their masters.

The path began a gentle slope down to the water, the brush opening up to reveal the riverbank. They hurried forward, eager to leave the dense woods behind them. Palmer could make out a rudimentary dock ahead, exactly as Bentley had promised. This was where the River Rats tied up whenever they came to Wilcolme, separate from the town dock that no longer welcomed their kind. Palmer caught a glimmer of movement through the bushes to his right. He blinked, unsure if he'd seen an otter or just a trick of the light.

Something hummed like an angry wasp. Bentley gasped and crumpled, a crossbow bolt buried in his shoulder. The cold wind swirling around them abruptly stopped, and the light guiding their steps winked out.

Palmer and Layla dropped into a crouch, weapons pointed in the direction of their attacker. An eerie, keening cry rang through the woods behind them.

"Unseen!" Layla said, voice shaking.

Unseen behind them and at least one archer ahead. Palmer's mind raced. The mage had been using a concealment spell, so whoever shot him was firing blind, not caring who they hit—or if they hit anyone at all. The goal was simply to keep them from reaching the river.

Without Bentley's light, it was too dark to see detail. Palmer drew out his lighter, working by feel to find the mechanism that activated it. With a whirr, the thing flared. Shielding the flame, Palmer sprang to Bentley's side, pausing long enough to ensure the mage was still breathing. Just barely. The short, thick bolt was —like most from Wilcolme Haven—fletched with ordinary goose feathers. Palmer knew better than to pull it from the wound and cause more bleeding, but he snapped the shaft closer to the wound. It was something every child of the haven learned to do.

Palmer cast a quick glance at Layla. "Cover me. We'll make for the water."

She scanned the forest. "Who fired on us?"

"Townsfolk."

"What? We left them behind when we entered the forest."

Palmer put his lighter away, aware the flame would make

them a target. He heaved Bentley upright and slung the man across his shoulders. The mage was more solid than he looked. "My guess is they circled back to the town dock and sailed here to intercept us."

"How do you know?"

"Because the shot came just as we reached the edge of the forest." He started for the water's edge as fast as his burden would allow.

Layla matched his pace. "Do they want to capture us or kill us?"

"They want to keep us in the forest to die. Clearly, they don't know Bentley is with us, or that he's injured. They'd never risk his life."

The obvious thing was to call out, to tell their attackers they were firing on their own mage. But then the eerie hunting cry of the Unseen came again much, much closer. The scent of Bentley's blood would be a magnet to the monsters.

Palmer broke into a stumbling run, praying that he'd keep his feet. More bolts hummed, burying themselves in the sand and rocks around him. Layla's pistol fired, and he heard the unearthly shriek of an Unseen as it dropped to the dirt behind them.

Palmer glanced over his shoulder in time to see a second creature scuttle through the trees toward them, eyes flashing in the flare of Layla's shot. The branch above the thing's head splintered, but it got away.

They had almost made it to the shore when a bolt scored Palmer's side. Heat shot through him, pain stealing his vision for a crucial second. The wound wasn't deep, but it tore skin and flesh. Sudden weakness made him stumble, but he managed to recover before Bentley slipped from his shoulders. He veered to his left, where boulders a few yards from the dock made them a more difficult target. Layla ducked behind the tallest rock, using it for cover. Palmer set Bentley on the ground, then doubled over, gasping at the pain in his side.

"There are three boats on the water," Layla reported. "One is right next to the bank. That's the one firing at us."

Palmer dragged himself up to peer over the rocks. Hot blood coursed down his side, but he pushed the pain aside enough to think. Thick clouds deepened the darkness, making the silhouettes of the two distant craft hard to see. Torches burned at the fore and aft of the closest vessel, showing men at the oars and others with their bows trained on the shore.

Layla sagged against the rock. "What do we do?" she murmured, her words almost lost beneath the lapping of the river. Fishing a handful of bullets from her pocket, she began reloading her pistol with the ease of long practice.

Palmer looked up and down the river, hoping to spot the sleek vessels of the River Rats, but there were none in sight. "Bargain. Bentley keeps the haven safe from the Unseen. They can't afford to lose him."

And, for all his troubled memories of the place, he wouldn't doom the people of the haven if it was in his power to save them. He bent over the mage, praying that he'd survived the trip to the water's edge. He still felt residual cold clinging to his limbs, indicating that Bentley's concealment spell was still partially active. A good thing, or the monsters would have swarmed them by now.

Palmer continued his examination. Bentley's breath rattled as if blood was seeping into his airways as well as coursing from the wound. Palmer tried packing his handkerchief around the wound, but it immediately soaked through. Ignoring the cold, he stripped off his waistcoat and then his shirt, using the latter to staunch Bentley's wound.

Despite the panic in her eyes, Layla still gave Palmer's torso an appraising look, one eyebrow cocked with a connoisseur's approval. "Do you want me to take off my petticoat?"

A dozen inappropriate comments crowded into his brain.

"For bandages, I mean," she added dryly, apparently reading his expression.

He didn't get the chance to reply. He pressed too hard on Bentley's wound, and the mage cried out for all that he seemed to be unconscious. The sound felt enormous in the uneasy dark.

It was time to play what cards he had. Palmer rummaged in Bentley's robes, finding his flask and upending the vile liquid on the feathers of a crossbow bolt. He took out his lighter, touching the flame to the feathers the instant before he shot it in the air. The flame flickered out as the bolt sped upward, then caught as it reached the apex of its flight. The sky bleached white in a flare of magic. There was no way that the men of Wilcolme Haven could mistake the signal for anything else. They would know the mage was in trouble—and therefore, the haven itself was at stake.

Thunder rumbled again, closer this time. A figure hurtled from the edge of the forest, bounding across the rocky shore of the river with inhuman speed. Palmer leaped to his feet, gripping his crossbow and putting himself between his friends and the Unseen. The creature sprang, crashing into Palmer and bearing him to the ground before he could get off a shot. Palmer fell to his back, his breath leaving in a convulsive rush as the Unseen pounced on his chest.

It raked the weapon from his hand, scraping it away along with flesh. Palmer bucked to no avail. Then the crushing weight shifted as the creature dug its claws into his flesh. Palmer's gasp dragged air back into his lungs, giving him enough strength to drive his fist into the creature's throat.

It rose up with a shriek of rage, giving Palmer a first real look at his foe. It had too many needle-like teeth, its lips insufficient to cover them all. Some protruded like tusks, others like wayward fangs glistening with drool. As the thing loomed over Palmer, its jaw dropped impossibly wide, as if it could unhinge like a snake's, and the Unseen reared to strike.

Palmer grabbed for its throat, catching the monster as it dove to bite. Its skin felt loose, as if its flesh had wasted despite its obvious strength. The creature's muscles corded, the instinct to bite stronger than the need to escape Palmer's stranglehold. He squeezed, his arms shaking with the effort to throttle his attacker and hold the dripping fangs away from his face. Saliva dripped onto his cheek, sliding wetly across his skin as the creature's rancid breath threatened to suffocate him.

A shot echoed off the nearby boulders. Palmer recognized the sound of Layla's pistol. The urge to protect her raked him as sharply as the Unseen's claws, but he could see nothing. He could guess, though—where there was one monster, there were always more.

The creature's claws found the arrow wound in his side, the filthy tips wriggling through the rent in his skin. Pain speared through him, shooting up his spine to the top of his skull. Palmer roared and heaved the monster over, agony giving him strength. He smashed the thing's skull against the rocky ground, stunning it long enough to pin it down.

He got a glimpse of Layla crouched over Bentley's still form, with her pistol cupped in an expert grip. Three monsters lay dead at the edge of the forest, evidence of her handiwork. She aimed at the space between the tree line and the shore where the Unseen were wading into the water and leering at the boats. Two more had fallen with bolts in their throats, but the temptation of so many edible humans just out of reach overcame their caution. Despite their hatred of water, some were in up to their waists.

The Unseen writhed in Palmer's grip, snapping its jaws on the air between them. Palmer was dimly aware of the boats drawing away from the shore and the monsters lurking there. If the Unseen gave up all hope of catching a floating dinner and began searching the area, they would find him and his party.

The Unseen on top of him arched up, sending Palmer tumbling across the hard ground. He rolled to his feet, ignoring flashes of pain that blanked his vision. He was losing strength along with his blood, and he was no match for the monster. A glance at the ground around him showed his bow was out of reach. The only hope he had was to keep the creature off balance.

Palmer rushed the Unseen, driving his shoulder into the beast hard enough to shove it across the rocky shore and topple it into the shallows of the river. Palmer went down on top of it, a knee in its gut, and forced it under the water. The cold waves stung Palmer's wounds, but he forced the sensation away. Killing this creature was the only way any of them would survive.

The Unseen thrashed beneath him. Palmer scrabbled with one hand, finding a fist-sized rock and smashing it down on the creature's skull. It bellowed in rage, swallowing water as it did and choking convulsively. Palmer struck again, nauseated by the crunch of bone. The Unseen struck out, digging claws into the bare flesh of Palmer's chest. They slid into the muscle, snaking through flesh. Palmer's lips parted, but the pain of breathing—of moving at all—was too much. He brought the rock down again, his vision swimming, turning dark and then white at the edges as the tension faded from the sinews of the Unseen's body.

One more strike of the rock, this time crushing through skull and brain. The monster stilled and Palmer slumped, the icy water caressing his agonized flesh. His eyes drifted shut, exhaustion threatening to pull him under unless he stayed in motion.

As he pushed to his feet, orange light licked across the water toward the shore. Unseen screamed in rage and pain.

Palmer jerked his head up, fatigue falling away.

The river was on fire.

CHAPTER 11

Layla adjusted her aim carefully, ignoring the bite of sharp rocks against her knees as she shifted her position. She'd been picking off Unseen stragglers who wandered too close for comfort. Even so, she only aimed for those at a distance from their fellows. She couldn't be sure how much of Bentley's concealment spell was still active, and gunshots attracted attention.

Fortunately, the Unseen were entirely focused on the haven's boats. Not even the scent of Bentley's blood was tempting them now—or it wouldn't as long as the breeze blew the right way. It was coming, thick with the smell of rain, from a storm in the west. If the wind changed, they were dead.

The Unseen in her sights was little more than a dozen yards away. It had paused, resting on all four limbs like a particularly ugly dog, and was sniffing the air. Had it caught the scent of Bentley's wound? She made a final calculation, lining up a bullet through its temple. Unseen were hard to kill, but a head shot would do it. She pulled the trigger.

It clicked, but nothing happened. With a gut-punch of dread, she realized the pistol had misfired. The Unseen turned at the sound, its bulbous eyes seeming to pierce the boulders where she hid. Layla shrank down, concentration slipping as she fumbled with the weapon.

Suddenly the chaos surrounding her pressed in—the shrieks of the Unseen down the shore, lunging for the boats, the splash of Palmer battling his opponent to her left, and the warbling cry of the monster she'd failed to kill. It was aware of her now, and it was hunting.

She'd held her courage tight until now, but it was threatening to dissolve like a sugar lump in boiling water. She scrabbled to her feet, aimed, and shot just as the Unseen bounded over the boulder where she'd crouched. Its chest exploded, but kept coming until she'd emptied two more shots in its skull.

Layla's limbs shook as she stared down at the twisted corpse. She allowed herself only a second before whirling around to Palmer, ready to assist. But he was rising from the water, the errant light highlighting the curves and hollows of his frame.

Something moved behind him, then fire licked across the water, missing the three boats filled with the haven's folk and rushing toward the Unseen. Those furthest into the water kindled and burned, flames engulfing them as if they were no more than straw. Those who had lagged behind shrieked as they scrambled for the riverbank, their cries muffled by the rumble of the coming storm.

Nothing burned in water. This was magic.

As she watched, four sleek, black boats emerged from the night, their oars lifted clear of the river's fiery surface. River Rats. She knew those craft—they docked within Londria's walls from time to time. Even there, they were feared.

The flames seemed to spread from the prow of the leading craft, where a man in a long coat held a silver cup aloft. From the cup came a thin stream of liquid that burned the instant it touched the waves. They were odd flames, less yellow than blue with peaks the same white as the burning bolt Palmer had shot into the air.

Like startled birds, the haven's ships turned, circling behind the newcomers and their fire to flee back toward the town. The shore was clear of Unseen. Layla's breath eased a degree. They were safe, at least until these newcomers came ashore. She should prepare. They might need to keep fighting.

Layla returned to Bentley's side, crouching beside his head. "Wake up."

The mage's eyes flickered open. "Who is it?" he asked in a rasping voice.

"Layla," she replied.

His face twisted with irritation. "No, not you. Who brought magefire? I can smell it."

Layla sniffed, but sensed nothing. "River Rats. I recognize their boats."

Bentley closed his eyes and exhaled a long sigh. "Let them know we're here."

"Are your spells still concealing us?"

"I'm afraid my strength has run out."

She'd suspected as much, but the news still chilled her bones. Layla rose to obey, but Palmer was already at the water's edge, waving at the lead ship. As the craft turned their way with the grace of a hawk, she went to Palmer's side. The flames on the water scattered, dancing over the waves until they winked out.

"I knew the River Rats had magic," she said, "but never anything like this." She realized her voice sounded strangely distant, as if she were commenting on the weather. Inside, her nerves hummed like a mechanism wound too tight.

Palmer turned her way, his face pale. It was then she saw the gashes in his skin weeping blood turned dark by the night. For a long moment, her heart seemed to stop.

"It's going to be all right," he said. "We're safe now."

She gave a hiccup of delayed fright and began to cry.

PALMER TOOK Layla in his arms. She melted against him, weeping with the whole-hearted abandon of a woman who had reached the end of her strength. Palmer didn't speak, but simply held her, breathing in the warm, salty scent of her skin.

The moment didn't last long. As abruptly as she'd started to weep, Layla was done. She drew away almost abruptly, wiping her eyes. "There's no time for this. You're wounded."

Palmer blinked. "It's nothing."

Which was true and not. He was alive, but the wound hurt like hell.

Her look said he was an idiot. "We'd best greet our new friends, Detective Inspector."

Palmer turned to follow her pointing finger. The first of the sleek, black crafts had drawn close to shore, and a handful of the River Rats were wading out to meet him and his friends. They carried torches, the flickering light playing over their aquiline features and loose-fitting clothes. The man leading the shore party was the same one who had set the river afire. He wore a gold torc around his neck, marking him as the captain of the small fleet. Beads studded his long, straight hair and the ends of his drooping mustache. A curved knife hung at his hip.

"We saw the mage's fire shot into the sky," he said, the words marked with a liquid accent. "Where is Bentley?"

Without a word, Palmer showed him to where Bentley lay in the shelter of the rocks. Layla—now perfectly composed—was with Bentley, mopping his blood away with what looked like a strip from her petticoat.

The captain gestured to two of his crew. "Get the mage on board."

They hastened to obey, lifting Bentley with a mix of efficiency and care worthy of well-trained medics. Palmer's anxiety eased a degree.

"I am Galpin, the leader of this family." He gestured to the sleek boats.

Palmer nodded. Among the River Rats, family referred to a group that traveled together as much as it did blood relations. These boats were only part of the fleet. Somewhere, there would be larger, slower vessels where they lived and raised their young.

"My name is Palmer, and this is Miss McHugh."

Galpin glanced at the gash in Palmer's side, then at the swirling ink where the fortune teller in the Riverside Bazaar had healed the Unseen's bite. "You have helped our people in the past."

"The Unseen have journeyed into my home city of Londria."

Galpin's dark eyebrows rose, as if this was news to him. "That mark tells us to give you our aid. Come, we will take you from this place."

"Thank you."

Layla drew a fistful of metal objects from her pocket and lifted one from the pile. It was a heavy gold pocket watch. "Will this pay for my passage?"

Galpin took the watch, turning it over in his palm to admire the case. "I would not leave you behind."

"I would not ask you to take me for nothing," she replied.

"This will fetch a good price. I accept the payment."

Palmer said nothing, though the flash of gold in the torchlight piqued his curiosity. Had it been Hardwin's? Or another mark's? The question lingered even if he was far too tired to give it voice.

Galpin slid the watch into a pocket inside his tunic and then plucked a ring of keys from the jumble in Layla's hand.

"So many locks to open," he said with a flash of white teeth. "Do you know what they all are?"

"No," Layla replied.

He dropped the keys back into her hand. "That is the way with so many of the land dwellers. Always too many answers, and never the right questions."

Layla opened her mouth to speak, then snapped it shut with a frown.

"Come then," Galpin beckoned. "The magefire will not frighten the Unseen for long."

Palmer took Layla's arm, steering her forward. They followed the captain, wading through the freezing water until they climbed aboard the boat. It was long and narrow, a little larger than the other two boats and with a small cabin at its center. The instant they were ready to sail, Galpin summoned an older woman who wore the same loose tunic and leggings as the other sailors.

"Tend to his wounds," Galpin ordered. "He has been marked as a friend."

With a brisk nod, the woman led Palmer into the cabin, leaving Layla with Bentley. Palmer glanced over his shoulder, reluctant to be separated. Then again, he felt better knowing she was there to watch over the mage.

"Sit," said the older woman as she steered Palmer through the cabin door.

There was a long, low table in the middle of the room, but no chairs. Uncertainly, he perched on the edge of the table. The woman didn't object as she spread a canvas roll lined with many pockets, each holding a tool. Palmer regarded the rows of needles, tweezers, and knives with a distinct lack of enthusiasm.

"Your last wound asked for a healing sigil," she said with a hint of amusement. "This is not so bad." With that, she bent to the task of threading a needle, her gray-streaked hair falling around her face.

"It feels bad. The thing dug its claws into me."

"Better claws than teeth."

Palmer's search for a reply was interrupted as Galpin entered the cabin. The captain leaned against the wall, folding his arms. With three people, the space was crowded.

"You and your woman are from the city," he said. "Why are you in the haven?"

Palmer hissed as the needle pierced his skin. "I am a detective inspector from Londria. I am looking for a suspect in a serious crime. I know he was in Wilcolme Haven earlier this night and looking for a means of escape. He is going by Polliver, although that might not be his true name."

Galpin shrugged. "We had a brother waiting with his boat tonight. The mage asked that he come here. We trade our supplies for Bentley's spells, like the magefire. As you saw tonight, such things are useful against the Unseen."

"What happened to your brother and his boat?" Palmer asked.

"He did not meet Bentley as we'd planned, and his boat was not where we expected it to be." Galpin's mouth flattened to a grim line. "Perhaps your fugitive reached him before the mage did."

"Could Polliver have hired him?"

"Unlikely, although that is the answer I hope for. Otherwise, my brother and his crew sailed against their will. That is less likely. We are not weak."

But Polliver had already blown up the *Leopard*. He was dangerous. "Polliver needs an airship. Where would he go?"

"Drakesford has a small airfield. My brother's boat could reach that by morning."

"Then that is where Polliver will want to go."

"Then once the mage is returned to his home, we shall go there also." Galpin straightened from his slouch against the wall. "I must ensure my brother is safe."

"Agreed," Palmer said, and the captain left.

Once she was done stitching, the woman smeared Palmer's injuries with the same nose-wrinkling paste the fortune teller had used back in Londria. Finally, she pulled a heavy linen shirt over his head, dressing him with the rough efficiency as she might a recalcitrant child. He was released back onto the deck with a shove and a pot of ointment for later.

Palmer rejoined Layla, who was kneeling beside Bentley. They had placed the mage on a thick layer of blankets atop a stretcher, and then covered him warmly. Bentley's eyes were closed and his breathing labored. Layla looked up as Palmer approached, her features drawn.

"They've done what they could," she said. "They say his best chance is the haven, where he can rest."

"He has to return," Palmer said, his heart heavy. "The wards won't hold without him."

"The sailors signaled one of the haven's boats while you were inside the cabin," she said. "They are coming to take him home."

As she spoke, a lantern flared to the starboard of the boat. A minute later, a beefy man boarded, wearing what looked like clothes suitable for a dinner party. He approached Bentley's makeshift bed, Galpin on his heels.

The newcomer regarded Layla and her bloodied gown warily. "Miss McHugh."

"Mr. Cartwright," she replied evenly.

Cartwright looked from Layla to Palmer, a glimmer of recognition in his eyes. "I remember you."

Palmer began to shrug, but his wounds protested. "We were boys. You're the butcher's son."

"The shop's mine now," Cartwright replied, somehow making that sound like a threat. "You might have been the schoolteacher if you hadn't put a knife in his heart."

"And the haven would be in a much better position if your townsfolk hadn't shot their own bloody mage." Palmer's temper slipped. "Let's stick to the problem in front of us."

"You've slipped the noose once too often. Now Hardwin is—"

"You have come for the mage," Galpin broke in. "That is the only person you will be taking from my craft."

"Are you sure about that?" the butcher shot back.

"Are you certain you should be testing me?" Galpin leaned forward an inch, but the shadows around him seemed to spread like wings.

Cartwright fell back a step, eying the captain warily. "Very well. Let's get down to business."

Galpin gave a curt nod. "Bentley is gravely wounded. He will need all the care your doctors can provide."

"We'll see to it," Cartwright replied. As he bent to assess the patient, he swept the others with a resentful glance. Then he gave the mage a poke with one beefy finger. "He's out cold."

"If Bentley does not recover, the haven must be evacuated," Palmer put in.

"I know that," the butcher muttered. "I've known that all my life, same as you." He signaled to another townsman, who stepped from the shadows behind him and took his place at the foot of the stretcher.

Galpin cleared his throat. "If the worst happens, the People of the River are prepared to extend their aid and mercy."

"No," Cartwright shot back before the captain was done speaking. "The mage is ours. The town is ours, and we have our own boats. We want nothing from the River Rats."

Palmer bridled. "Don't be an idiot."

But Galpin put a hand on Palmer's arm and gave a slow, stately nod. "We have heard and understood. What happens in Wilcolme Haven is the affair of its residents alone."

"You're damned right it is," Cartwright muttered.

∽

LAYLA WATCHED as the butcher lifted the head of the stretcher while the other townsman raised the foot. Layla bent down, kissing Bentley's forehead. "Good luck," she whispered. "Get well."

Bentley's eyes flickered open. For a moment, he seemed

confused, but then he gave her the smile of a wicked cherub. "Look after Palmer. He's an unfinished project, but he mostly means well."

She tried to smile, but it felt wobbly. "I'll do my best."

She stepped back to make room as Palmer squeezed Bentley's hand in farewell. "Thank you for your help yet again, old friend. You've always been my shield."

"Is it time to make my confession?" Bentley asked, his voice hoarse.

"Only you know that," Palmer replied. "That's a truth I can't face."

Bentley's eyes closed again for an instant, but then he roused, his gaze moving from Cartwright, to Galpin, to Layla, and then back to Palmer. "Then hear this. I slew Babbington."

"What?" Cartwright exclaimed, brow creasing in surprise.

"Wait—" Palmer began.

"We both know what he was," Bentley interrupted, putting a hand on Palmer's sleeve to silence him. "Men like Babbington flee to the havens because they have burned every other bridge. Here they can hide, because every single soul in this hell is nursing their private demons. No one asks questions."

There, Bentley ran out of breath, his chest laboring to find more air. They all remained silent until he could speak again. "I stopped him from hurting more children, for his sake as well as theirs."

With that, the mage fell silent and did not speak again, though his breath continued to rattle in and out. Layla blinked hard and smoothed the hair from Bentley's forehead.

"Blood and thunder," Cartwright breathed as he caught Palmer's gaze. "Then why did he let you take the blame?"

Palmer's face twisted. Layla couldn't tell if it was grief, anger, or both.

"Perhaps because you were gone?" she suggested. "There was no sign you would ever be back."

"Well, the town will deal with this once he's fit," Cartwright concluded. "Best get Bentley off this Rat boat and under the care of a proper doctor."

Palmer pressed the mage's hand one last time and stepped back, his face chalk-white in the light of the boat's lanterns. Cartwright and his friend carried the mage to the haven's boat. Then the two crafts parted ways.

Layla joined Palmer where he stood, watching the town's last lights vanish into the night. She could feel his warmth like a balm. "What will happen to Bentley?"

Palmer swallowed, anger pulling at the corners of his mouth. "I don't know. Under ordinary circumstances, not even a mage can escape the consequences of a confession like that, but the town relies on his talents."

Layla slipped her arm through his, sharing more of his marvelous warmth. "I'm sorry."

He didn't say more, and they drifted in silence, side by side and wrapped in their own troubled thoughts. What was Palmer feeling? Bentley had called himself a friend and yet waited until his deathbed to clear Palmer's name. Then again, he'd helped them through the forest to the river.

No one was entirely good or bad.

She hoped someone, someday would think the same of her.

~

PALMER WAS content to stand by the rail, Layla at his side, and watch the night slip away. Fatigue drowned his thoughts, but he was aware of the sentries on either side of the boat, watching for the creatures lurking in the dark. The River Rats knew the waters better than anyone, knew the sandbars and rapids that could drive a boat and its passengers into the open mouths of the Unseen. They took no chances.

A quarter hour later, brilliant lights filled the sky in showers of blues and violets, like the sparklers from a children's party. Like fireworks and celebration, except it wasn't. This was magic unleashed. Wilcolme's wards had failed—all of them, all at once, releasing their power in one wild flood.

Bentley was dead.

Palmer closed his eyes and tried not to imagine what happened next.

CHAPTER 12

As dawn broke, Captain Galpin left Palmer and Layla at Drakesford, stopping only long enough for them to disembark at the dock near the airfield. Though their parting was warm, with many thanks on Palmer and Layla's side, the captain had other concerns. The River Rats had not spotted their missing boat, and their next order of business was to mount a search.

Palmer watched the slim, black vessel leave, the prow a sharp silhouette against the grays and pinks of the dawn-painted river. His senses told him it was a magnificent sight, but his emotions were still frozen, like a rabbit hiding from a fox.

But he was police, trained to function when a reasonable person could not. He led Layla away from the dock, momentarily glad they had no luggage. They had to pass through Drakesford proper to reach the airfield, and so their path led through the arched town gate, which was topped with an enormous wooden dragon painted a vibrant green. Unlike Wilcolme Haven, this town and its surrounding fields were enclosed by a high fence that marked the perimeter of the wards. This was more like Londria, where the lines of safety were clearly drawn. The mage here was no Bentley, who had ignored every protocol the Conclave demanded.

The memory of his friend, and all he had done, tightened Palmer's throat. With a strange sense of dislocation, he realized news of Wilcolme's fall hadn't spread yet. The locals here were setting up booths and table for a market. Baskets of fish vied for attention with bundles of early greens, and the bakery lads were carrying trays piled with fresh pies. Drakesford was a trading hub in these remote lands, and that prosperity showed.

"Is there someone we should tell?" Layla asked. "About what happened at Wilcolme?"

He considered. "No. We're still looking for Polliver. News like that will draw attention, and it's better if we can take him by surprise."

"Then what do we do?"

"Do you still have the gallery case?"

She touched the reticule fastened to the belt of her ruined dress. "I do."

"Good. Then we show his picture and ask a few quiet questions on our way to the airfield. It's the only place here he's likely to go."

Layla produced the gallery case, which had been badly dented at some point, and only got it open after a struggle with the catch. They showed Polliver's picture at every stall that had been set up so far that day, but no one recognized his face. That confirmed Palmer's suspicion that his quarry had landed before dawn and gone straight to the airfield, or he hadn't landed at all.

Eventually, they gave up on the market and walked the long path to the airfield's ticket office. Layla produced enough cash to purchase passage home for both of them. Palmer's funds had been confiscated at the jail, so he was forced to accept a loan.

Neither spoke much beyond the necessary. Palmer's mood remained muffled, as if a thick layer of gauze separated him from the world at large. A sole thought tolled like a funeral bell, over and over. Wilcolme Haven was gone. When the mage failed, the wards failed, and the forest took back its land by tooth and claw. The havens—even cheerful Drakesford—were a cheat, a magic trick that produced good for cities the townsfolk would never visit.

Thank the gods he and Layla—and Kieran—had left in time.

"Why didn't Cartwright accept help with an evacuation?" Layla asked, as if she'd been reading Palmer's thoughts. "Didn't he know what might happen?"

"Every citizen of the havens knows what will happen if the wards fall."

"Then I really don't understand." She paused to shade her eyes from the sun. A small transport ship was coming in for landing, the balloons striped green and blue. It flew the colors of Stonegate, a city to Londria's north.

Palmer followed the ship's gentle downward drift. "That idiot Cartwright should have grabbed at the captain's offer of help instead of falling back on his distrust of the River Rats. And yet, the human preserves sanity by denying the worst will ever happen."

"Couldn't Captain Galpin go to the haven anyway?"

They resumed walking. "Galpin couldn't force Cartwright—or anyone else in Wilcolme—to be smart. The town was hostile to the Rats. If they approached, the watch would likely fire on them. Besides, one of Galpin's vessels and its crew are missing. That would be his first concern."

And once the slaughter had begun, there was nothing Galpin or anyone else could do. The havens could be ugly in a way outsiders didn't fathom.

Palmer had no allegiance to Wilcolme, no love or even liking for its people. But no sane person could imagine an entire town swallowed—literally—by the Unseen without violent revulsion. Those emotions would hit him once he was in his own home, with a glass of whisky and perfect privacy. Then he would grieve, let memory and feeling flood back into his soul. For now, he was hollowed out, as empty as if his past had vanished along with the place. That was how it had to be until his mission was complete.

Nevertheless, by the time they'd approached the eatery that served the airfield's passengers, hunger penetrated Palmer's mental fog. Regardless of events, the body kept burning fuel, and his last proper meal had been—he was no longer sure.

The cafe was in a small, squat building at the edge of the airfield. The windows had steamed up in the cool morning air, so their first proper view of the tables came when they pushed through the double doors and were greeted by the scent of bacon and gravy. Layla started toward the counter where customers ordered food, but Palmer caught her elbow.

"Wait," he said, keeping his voice low.

"What for?" She looked around in confusion, then caught her breath. "Surely it can't be that easy."

"I wouldn't call everything we've been through easy, would you?"

She didn't reply, but stared at the corner table with its lone occupant. A pink flush darkened her cheekbones while her mouth thinned to a flat, angry line. "There are too many innocents nearby to open fire."

"Just as well," Palmer replied. "Even when the Conclave was active, questioning a corpse rarely went well."

He approached the table at a casual amble, his hands in his pockets. Polliver, in a dreadful mustard-colored suit—sat with his hat pulled low, shoveling food into his mouth as if he hadn't eaten in days. He looked up as Palmer slid into the chair beside him, blocking his escape.

"Excuse me," he protested loudly, setting down his fork.

"No," Palmer replied. "I don't."

A few heads turned at the sound of raised voices. Palmer gave the other patrons a reassuring smile and continued speaking in a lower tone. "I take it your presence here means the craft you arrived on has sailed safely away?"

"Of course," Polliver stammered. "Why wouldn't they? I paid them well."

No sooner had he stopped speaking than a look of dismay washed over his face. Most likely, Palmer had startled him into giving a straight answer. One that revealed too much.

Layla took the chair across the table and leaned forward, pointedly scanning his features. "I wondered how you would appear up close. You're younger than I expected."

"Who are you?" Polliver demanded. "You look like vagabonds."

Palmer left him guessing a moment longer while he finally took a good look at the man. He had a forgettable face, soft and small-featured, but it had matured over the years—enough that Palmer hadn't recognized it from a distance. Moreover, photographs hadn't captured his furtive expression. It was that anxious twist of the mouth that triggered Palmer's memory now.

"He wasn't always Polliver," he said, addressing Layla. "His real name is Sam Gregory. He was a few years behind my brother in school."

Sam Gregory had been the youngest in a family of eight or nine children, the barefoot runt in a litter scrambling for survival. Since that time, he'd apparently clawed his way into a criminal organization. Things were going well enough for him that now he had shoes.

Recognition dawned in the man's eyes. "Liam Palmer. I know you."

Polliver reached inside his coat, but Palmer was there first, removing the pistol with professional ease. "Don't be naughty."

Polliver made to rise, but Palmer caught his wrist, pulling him up short. "A few things have changed since we last met. Now I'm Detective Inspector Palmer, Londria police. I'm arresting you on suspicion of sabotage of the airship *Leopard*."

The man tried to twist away. Palmer gripped the back of his jacket, hauled him to his feet, and turned him face-first to the wall. Palmer had lost his handcuffs along the way, but he had a stout rope from Galpin's boat. He bound Polliver's hands, then searched him for any more weapons. He pocketed a knife and, with a slight twinge of conscience, several cigarettes.

By the time he turned Polliver around, the other patrons were watching with extreme curiosity. A few left in haste.

"What's happening?" asked a heavy-set man in a mechanic's uniform. He rose from his table, a heavy spanner in one hand.

"This is a police matter," Palmer replied. "I'm removing a fugitive from your fair town. An escort to our ship would be appreciated."

The mechanic stroked his wiry gray whiskers. "With pleasure. We see too many questionable folk come and go from here."

"Thank you," Palmer said, bidding a mental farewell to breakfast.

"You're an idiot," Polliver retorted, low enough so that only Palmer could hear. "Why do you think I returned to Wilcolme Haven to see your brother? Aren't you curious to know where he fits into this affair? Let me go, and I'll tell you everything. Make it worth your while."

Palmer's breath caught. He yearned for those answers, but he'd heard such promises before. The Pollivers of the world would say anything to avoid punishment. "I'm sure the captain of our transport will allow early boarding, especially for the *Leopard*'s saboteur. You sent an entire crew of aeronauts to their deaths."

The bystanders overheard, and an angry murmur spread across the room. At least half the room wore flight uniforms. The mechanic folded his massive arms.

Polliver struggled with the desperation of a trapped animal, but was no match for Palmer's grip.

Layla pushed her pistol to the man's temple. "If you get the urge to run, just remember I'm not the police, and I don't play by their rules."

Polliver's eyes rolled in Layla's direction, the whites visible. Palmer marched him out of the building, Layla and the mechanic on either side. They strode across the dew-soaked grass, Palmer holding tight to his captive. If nothing else, he finally had something to show for the bloody debacle of this trip.

∽

ONCE ABOARD, Layla fell out of love with airships as quickly as she'd been smitten. The journey home was long and uncomfortable, made more so by Polliver's presence. The man was locked in a supply closet in the ship's cabin with Palmer standing guard. After a brief turn around the deck, Layla took a seat inside and pretended to sleep. She was hungry, tired, and dirty. Between homicidal town officials and flesh-eating monsters, she clearly wasn't cut out for country life.

Now her mind wouldn't stop racing, image after image flapping through her brain like startled birds. The best she could do was shoo them into a corner for later examination. Some were afterimages, imprints of stark emotion that she would hopefully come to terms with given time. There were others—like the whole keys and locks discussion on Captain Galpin's boat—that required a mental effort she couldn't manage at the moment. She wanted time to speed up so she could get home. She also wanted it to slow down so she could absorb everything that was happening.

But there was one thing she could be sure of. She had been tested under pressure and survived, and that was worth something. She wondered what Mrs. Randall would make of her story.

She jerked awake when Palmer touched her shoulder. Despite everything, exhaustion had swamped her.

"We've landed," he said.

Layla sat up, pushing the hair from her face. She'd all but given up trying to look tidy. A glance around told her the cabin was empty except for them—and Polliver in the storage closet. Everyone else was gathering on deck to disembark. "This is it, then. The end."

Palmer sat next to her. Fatigue ringed his eyes and etched lines at the corners of his mouth. "It's been a challenge I don't care to repeat."

She knew exactly what he meant, but she'd hoped for a different response. "Well, you're safely on the right side of the bars again."

He allowed a faint smile. "Back to being the law, you mean. I've let a few things slide during our country retreat."

Layla held his gaze, reading the subtle reminder there. He was the detective; she was the criminal. They'd been in a different time and place for a moment, but now things would return to their rightful order.

"Hardwin?" she asked.

The name hung in the air, silencing them both. Palmer could arrest her for murder. Every scrap of evidence was buried in the grave of Wilcolme Haven, but he knew the truth. And Palmer was the law in a way few police were.

He rose, as if he remembered an urgent appointment. "Don't remind me that happened."

So, he would leave it hanging over her head, like the sword in the fable, ready to slice when she least expected it. Fatigue had frayed her nerves too much to let that stand. "Don't forget Babbington."

He froze, suddenly dangerous. It was something in the way he held himself. The way he'd been on the shore of the river, battling the Unseen with his bare hands. "What do you mean?"

A bubble of apprehension rose inside her, but she rammed it down. "Bentley absolved you with his deathbed confession. A final gift. But it wasn't true."

He gathered himself inward, his cool mask slipping back into place. "What makes you think that?"

"The way you were in your cell," she said, a little surprised to hear a tremor in her voice. "You'd all but given up. I could imagine you furious or scheming, but never in despair. Unless you were actually guilty, of course. That's why you didn't want to see your brother. You couldn't face him."

Palmer had gone pale. The guilt in his eyes hurt her heart.

"The mage lied," he said.

"You had a chance at survival. Both you and Bentley knew he didn't."

"You're right, of course."

"Why did you do it?"

He paused, as if the words were hard to find. "Babbington found out I planned to leave the haven. He said Marvelle was too old to take a student. He threatened to end Kieran's apprenticeship and bring him back to the school. I couldn't let that happen."

"I see."

And they were even, secret for secret, but she wouldn't put that into words. Nor would she tell Mrs. Randall. Layla was a spy, sent on this mission to gather secrets, but this was different. This wasn't her tale to share. "I'm not going to ruin you. You had to save your brother."

He didn't answer.

"Is that why you became a policeman?"

He shrugged. "I owed my soul a debt."

Layla shook her head. "You'll die in the traces trying to make things right, Liam Palmer. That's worth more than the letter of the law."

Silence fell, because no conversation could follow without sounding unbearably trite. Layla turned away, unable to look him in the face. Then she remembered he'd loaned her his coat. She shrugged it off and handed it back.

"Thank you. Whatever you may think, you're a good man."

∼

HE TOOK the coat as she turned and walked away. Her scent clung to the garment, lemony and soft. It was a light, sunny counterpoint against the dark weight inside him. Logic said that he should be afraid that she knew the truth about his past. And yet, he wasn't. Layla was herself—chaotic, defiant, and occasionally lawless—but she would keep her word. She redefined the moral high ground in a way few could understand.

Whereas he had pursued a career in solving all crimes but the one he had committed. He continued to repay that debt with long hours and bad pay. He always would—perhaps running from truth, perhaps battling it to a truce. He wasn't sure any longer. He had an unrelenting supply of guilt, and Londria offered endless opportunity for atonement.

It would have to be enough. For now, he had to deliver Polliver to a jail cell and then find Kieran. If Bentley was right, his brother was somewhere in Londria, and he had information about the *Leopard*'s destruction. Polliver would talk—Palmer would see to that—but he was only one piece of a larger puzzle. However long it took him, Palmer would unmask the author of the *Leopard*'s demise.

As for how Bentley—or anyone else—had known the truth about Babbington's death? Well, Bentley had magic on his side, but the town fathers had no such claim. Had they made a lucky guess, or had there been a witness? He'd probably never know.

Footfalls approached the cabin—an even, determined march. Palmer approached the cabin door to see who it was and instantly recognized airfield security. The men bore the gold feather insignia of Fletcher Industries, the company who owned this airship.

"Captain Higgins tells us you have a prisoner to detain," said the leader. He was a spare man who looked as if he hadn't laughed in the last decade. "We've sent a runner to Gryphon Avenue for transport to your cells."

"He's in there." Palmer pointed to the supply closet door. "He's as slippery as they come."

A less experienced officer might be tempted to reveal more, but if these men knew what Polliver had done, there was a decent chance he'd never make it to the station. This was the *Leopard*'s home base.

The leader of the security detail gave a brief nod. "I give you my personal guarantee he will arrive at your cells in good order."

"That's all I need to hear."

After a few formalities, Palmer left the ship. It was evening, and the cold, wet March wind was a slap against his skin. It was hard to believe less than a week had passed since he'd left the city.

Layla stood a few dozen yards away. Her posture was uncertain, as if she was wondering what to do next. Palmer approached, worried that now she had no coat. Her dress was stained and torn, her hair straggling loose over her shoulders. She was barely recognizable as the gem of Hellion House.

"Would you like someone to escort you home?"

She looked up at him, her mouth quirking at one corner. "How chivalrous."

"Thank you," he said dryly.

He was tired—oh, so tired and simply laid flat. But there was a light in her that lifted those feelings, gently setting them aside. Had he ever truly noticed that before? Or had he looked no further than her astonishing beauty?

Before he knew what he was doing, he kissed her. Instinct demanded more than a polite brush of the lips, and he didn't waste the opportunity. Her mouth was soft and hot, her hair scented with the clean tang of the river breeze. He wanted more, but they were too visible in the middle of the airfield. Reluctantly, he stepped back.

"What was that for, Detective Inspector?" she asked archly.

"A thank you for all your assistance," he said, fumbling for words to cover the heat in his pulse. "You're an excellent partner in a tight spot. I'll fight at your side anytime."

Her eyes widened, gently mocking. "How enormously romantic."

He cleared his throat, feeling foolish. "No one has ever accused me of that." He took his coat off again, draping it over her shoulders.

She laughed, bright and merry, and looped an arm through his. "Nonsense. Ladies love being told they're good in a fight."

They strolled toward the path that led to the airfield gates.

"May I escort you home?" he asked.

She gave a soft sigh. "The last time we walked anywhere in this city, you arrested me."

"It led to some interesting outcomes."

"Agreed," she said. "But there is something to be said for variety."

"Meaning?"

"We can't battle a wilderness of monsters *every* time." She leaned into him, a soft weight against his side. "I ruined a perfectly good dress. Perhaps we could try dinner. Or a play."

∽

The action continues in *Queen's Tide*.

AFTERWORD

Thank you so much for joining me on this journey with Layla and Palmer. While this story answers some questions, it raises others. Where is Palmer's brother? And while we know the identity of the saboteur who destroyed the *Leopard*, who hired him? Most important of all, how do the events of this adventure impact the future? We're back in Londria with the Fletcher family for the next story, where a murder at the university takes center stage. I promise more airships, dragons, and a generous helping of suspects.

Read More from Emma Jane Holloway

www.EmmaJaneHolloway.com

When you visit the site, be sure to join the newsletter for a free, subscribers-only Hellion House prequel story and receive behind-the-scenes updates and previews of new Hellion House books.

FORTUNE'S EVE

A HELLION HOUSE SHORT STORY

Not all monsters dwell in the woods.

. . .

The mages of the Conclave have questions—dangerous ones that put airship pilot Gideon Fletcher and his sister, Miranda, in the midst of an inquisition for illegal magic.

The Fletchers live in an elegant world of gentlemen's clubs and Society balls, but their claim to fame is making daring rescues in the perilous Outlands. It's all fun and monsters until they save a man wanted by the Conclave, and the mages turn their suspicions toward Gideon's family.

Their scrutiny brings a new kind of peril. Little does Gideon know his sisters have much to hide. Trouble has arrived for the Fletchers, and it clearly means to stay.

For those who like steampunk adventure with a touch of magic—not to mention conspiracy, monsters, airships, and an adorable baby dragon.

SCORPION DAWN

A HELLION HOUSE NOVELLA

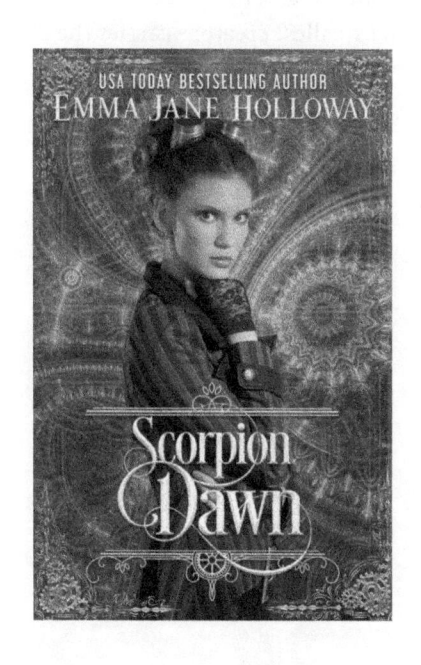

When the prey becomes the hunter ...

Miranda Fletcher lives in a glittering world of aeronauts and artists, dance cards and dandies, but terror lurks outside the city walls. The countryside is infested with hungry abominations called the Unseen, and a single crack in the capital's defenses invites disaster.

Then Miranda witnesses a murder and learns the walls aren't as secure as their magical protectors claim. But despite a string of bloody crimes, no one is foolhardy enough to question the mages, much less battle monsters at the gate.

Except Miranda. When tragedy shatters her home, she'll risk everything to get answers—and vengeance.

Sometimes the smallest creature carries the deadliest sting.

LEOPARD ASCENDING

A HELLION HOUSE NOVEL

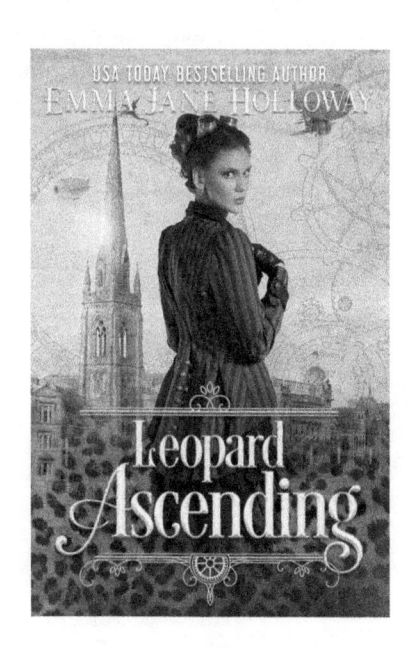

When courage and a crack shot aren't enough

After violence shatters Miranda Fletcher's world, she swears to protect those she loves. An air captain's daughter, she has courage enough to battle hungry monsters. Now a different threat hides among them—one much harder to destroy.

Miranda seeks out her rebel brother, Gideon, for aid. A private inquiry agent, he's searching for victims no one else dares to find. When one of his father's airships is blown from the sky, Gideon suspects his cases are linked to the disaster, and his family is the villain's new target.

Danger hides everywhere—in gaslit clubs and drawing rooms, in the secret halls of the mages, and among the monsters of the forest. Uncovering the city's dire truth could cost Miranda and Gideon their lives—or condemn them to a fate more terrible than the grave.

ALSO BY EMMA JANE HOLLOWAY

Hellion House Series

Fortune's Eve

Scorpion Dawn

Leopard Ascending

Hellion's Journey

Queen's Tide

Hellion Afternoon

Baskerville Affair series

A Study in Silks

A Study in Darkness

A Study in Ashes

The Baskerville Tales

The Baskerville Affair Complete Series

Audiobook

A Study in Silks

A Study in Darkness

A Study in Ashes

PRAISE FOR EMMA JANE HOLLOWAY

Magic, machines, mystery, mayhem, and all the danger one expects when people's loves and fears collide.

— KEVIN HEARNE

Holloway takes us for quite a ride, as her plot snakes through an alternative Victorian England full of intrigue, romance, murder, and tiny sandwiches.

— NICOLE PEELER, THE JANE TRUE SERIES

As Sherlock Holmes' niece, investigating murder while navigating the complicated shoals of Society—and romance—in an alternate Victorian England, Evelina Cooper is a charming addition to the canon.

— JACQUELINE CAREY

Splendid... the characters are thoroughly charming and the worldbuilding is first-rate

— ROMANTIC TIMES BOOK REVIEWS

Holloway stuffs her adventure with an abundance of characters and ideas and fills her heroine with talents and graces, all within a fun, brisk narrative.

— PUBLISHERS WEEKLY

ABOUT THE AUTHOR

Ever since childhood, USA Today Bestselling Author Emma Jane Holloway refused to accept that history was nothing but facts prisoned behind the closed door of time. Why waste a perfectly good playground coloring within the timelines? Accordingly, her novels are filled with whimsical impossibilities and the occasional eye-blinking impertinence—but always in the service of grand adventure.

Struggling between the practical and the artistic—a family tradition, along with ghosts and a belief in the curative powers of shortbread—Emma Jane has a degree in literature and job in finance. She lives in the Pacific Northwest in a house crammed with black cats, books, musical instruments, and half-finished sewing projects. In the meantime, she's published articles, essays, short stories, and novels, including *The Baskerville Affair* novels, featuring the niece of Sherlock Holmes, and the *Hellion House Series*.

Hellion's Journey © 2024 Naomi Lester

All rights reserved under the International and Pan-American Copyright Conventions. No part of this book may be reproduced or transmitted in any form or by any means, electronic or mechanical, including photocopying, recording, or by any information storage and retrieval system, without permission in writing from the publisher.

This is a work of fiction. Names, places, characters and incidents are either the product of the author's imagination or are used fictitiously, and any resemblance to any actual persons, living or dead, organizations, events or locales is entirely coincidental.

Warning: the unauthorized reproduction or distribution of this copyrighted work is illegal. Criminal copyright infringement, including infringement without monetary gain, is investigated by the FBI and is punishable by up to 5 years in prison and a fine of $250,000.

Cover by Sly Fox Cover Designs

Editing by Jacqui Nelson

www.ingramcontent.com/pod-product-compliance
Lightning Source LLC
LaVergne TN
LVHW042134290625
814993LV00026B/225